OBERON'S CHILD

Faith is wilful and beautiful and loves her mother, Prudence, dearly. However, she hates the man she calls 'Father'. Oberon Wild is a proud, overbearing man who succeeded in making a fortune through his mill, but who failed at the one thing he wanted more than anything — to sire a son and heir. How then will Faith escape from an unwanted engagement, protect her mother from Oberon's wrath and ultimately be with Benjamin, the man she loves?

VALERIE HOLMES

OBERON'S CHILD

Complete and Unabridged

LINFORD
Leicester

First published in Great Britain in 2006

First Linford Edition
published 2007

British Library CIP Data

Holmes, Valerie
    Oberon's child.—Large print ed.—
Linford romance library
    1. Love stories
    2. Large type books
    I. Title
    823.9'2 [F]

    ISBN 978–1–84617–719–4

1

Prudence stood nervously by the door of Wildermill Hall. Her husband, Oberon Wild, placed his hat on his head, straightened his jacket before his man slipped his greatcoat over it. He stared at his reflection in the looking glass and held his head high so that his chin did not look slack. He adjusted his cravat and made a *humph* sound, which intonated that he was content with his appearance for the day.

'You look very smart, Oberon,' Prudence said quietly.

'Would you ever expect me to look anything less, Mrs Wild? A man's appearance reveals his character to the world; one should always look one's best.' He cast a very critical and cursory look down at her plain navy gown. 'Now make sure you have your extra soup mid-morning. You must keep up your strength now.' He stood in front of her.

She tilted her head up as if expecting a kiss, but he merely shook his head dismissively. Only four months of marriage and she had displeased him already. No matter what she did, it was never good enough.

He criticised her decisions in front of the household servants, weakening her position and strengthening his. Such a short time for her to build up a resentment towards him, yet even she had to admit it was rapidly turning into a feeling much more sinful — hatred.

'Not in front of the servants, woman!' he rebuked her, then sighed. Prudence looked down dejectedly. 'You must learn some propriety. Did your mother not instruct you in these matters?' he asked her in a lowered voice and Prudence flushed deeply as she stared at the floor. The door was closed behind him after he left.

Prudence raised her head high, a tear in her eye, as she made her way back to the morning room. It was the room that seemed to capture the most sun. It offered her peace and a lightening of her spirits. At least the rest of the day was hers, until he returned in the evening.

Mr Oberon Wild mounted his horse, left his estate and rode along the country road that led him to the fashionable end to town. Then the scenery changed dramatically to the murky narrow cobbled way that was Prince Street. It meandered through the growing mill town, which he surveyed with pride.

The respectable new terraces behind them, they now travelled through the old mill town cottages as they, in turn, gave way to the new cheaper housing, which had been hastily erected for the workers. The air stank with the effluent from man and machine as the mill churned out both muck and money in what once had been an attractive farmed valley.

'Good day, sir.' A man in a large grubby greatcoat greeted him. Unlike his own immaculate appearance the man looked as though he had not washed for a month. He was sitting upon a sturdy looking mount and held a rifle loosely across his lap.

'Yes, Dermid, today you are correct in your assumption. It is a good day.' Oberon Wild did not stop to chat, as he was a man of few words, but kept riding past him. Dermid kicked his own horse onwards, falling into step behind, always watching the streets and anyone loitering near them as he protected his master's back.

The streets were as dark as the cramped houses erected along their sides. But through Oberon's eyes he saw only beauty, and he was pleased at the progress the town had made over the last three years.

For in his mind he praised himself for his compassion as he had provided homes for his people. If they chose to turn their new homes into hovels, then that was their affair; he had done his duty.

'Mornin', Mr Wild,' the greeting was shouted out from the blacksmith's shop. Josiah O. Baxter's name was written above the workshop door.

Oberon nodded slightly in the man's direction, hardly turning his head. Baxter was a good man, hard working and he was loyal to him.

He knew on which side his bread was buttered.

Oberon touched the rim of his hat with the end of his crop. It wasn't much of gesture, but it was enough to acknowledge the man. Baxter had had his uses after all.

Wild rode his horse onwards. There were many faces that turned away from him as he passed by, or looked up sullenly at his face. Still, what did he know or care about their deprivations, the shared privies and wells, they were not his concern, making money was, and that he was very good at. Families shared these buildings, sometimes ten to a room, but that made economical sense. It was not Oberon's life or lot.

He pictured his new fashionable country house, Wildermill Hall, in the large landscaped estate on the edge of town, and smiled to himself. He had designed and named it himself. Behind high walls and ornate gates his world was far removed from the grim reality of the townsfolk who he now rode by.

A scruffy blond-haired boy in a raggedy outfit stared blankly back at him from the street. He stepped out in front of them. Instantly Dermid lifted his rifle and rode alongside Wild, his eyes scanning the streets for signs of trouble. For a moment Oberon paused, not out of concern, but there was something about the intensity of the young lad's glare that surprised him.

'Ma's dead!' the boy shouted, his voice wavering as tears silently ran down his grubby cheeks.

'These things happen!' Oberon snapped back awkwardly and kicked his horse on walking it around the boy's thin figure. He glanced at Dermid, which was all the instruction the man needed to remove the brat from his path.

'Pa says you killed her . . . in there . . . why?' the child shouted his question as he pointed towards the mill. Before Dermid could ride the boy off the street he was swiftly picked up in a man's arms. The boy was still pointing towards the mill but his voice drifted off as he was carried off down an alley.

'Do you want me to give the brat a thorough beating or should I find the brat's father, Mr Wild?' Dermid asked hopefully.

'No man. Not today . . . next time, perhaps.'

Dermid dropped back a step. A look of disappointment crossed his face, which did not go unnoticed by Wild.

Oberon paid no heed to him. If he saw the lad again he'd have him taken to the poorhouse and his father punished for such mutinous talk. It was just as well for them that he was in high spirits this morning and the rabble was not going to spoil it.

He passed by the poor, the cold, the starving without compassion. He paused momentarily as he saw one of the Wesleyan's preacher men entering a worker's house. The man had the audacity to stand on the threshold and turn around to face him.

He removed his hat in a gesture of what Oberon took to be mock respect.

'Good morning, Mr Wild.' The preacher walked forward to greet him.

'Morning it is, good it maybe, however there work to be done,' Oberon answered abruptly.

'Indeed, and it is the Lord's work that I should like to speak to you about, sir. May I have a few moments of your time to discuss . . .'

'No!' was Oberon's abrupt response. 'Time is precious and I suggest you stop wasting yours!' He trotted away. Dermid glared back at the preacher as he followed on.

'Trouble makers and beggars,' Oberon muttered under his breath, that's what they were in his eyes; always asking for more and more. Time was money. The man was not of the true church anyway. He'd soon put paid to his meddling and that would be that. He would not have any of them in this town. For rabble-rousing was what he thought it was.

Without his mill and his housing, they would all starve. If they didn't like it, they were free to leave and take their heretic with them; then the others would realise how fortunate they were to have work whilst many men had none, his mill-workers had homes and jobs.

If they could not look after their own brats then they should stop having them. To Oberon the answer to all other people's problems was simple. They should work until providence decided their fate.

He looked down from his thorough-bred with pride at what he had achieved within his lifetime and felt nothing but loathing at the ungrateful wretches who worked for him in equal measure. His expensive overcoat and highly polished boots protected him against the penetrating cold. The damp air caressed his clean cheeks but did not travel down his neck beyond his tightly fastened cravat.

The raggedy people he passed by, grey of face and thin and stooped in stature were of little importance to Oberon. They were to him his future and would one day be the inheritance of his son. But he cared nothing for the individual man, woman or child just so long as there was a plentiful supply of hands to keep his mill working around the clock.

God was good to him, for with the depression he had made sure that the plentiful supply of labour was there for him and cheap too. From every dark cloud Oberon prided himself that he could make a silver lining. It was all down to how you thought. Oberon 'thought' a lot. He was pleased he had been born a man who had a particularly astute reasoning.

Emotions and conscience did not mix with business. He had clarity of purpose unlike the feather-headed woman he had had to marry. But Prudence had quite a substantial amount of money and respectability to her name so his sacrifice was, he supposed, worth it.

At least she was quiet and listened to him, although he doubted she under-stood a word he said. His father would have been so proud of him; a mill, a wife, and, in a few more months, a son. Soon his world would be complete.

He prided himself on being an astute businessman. He spent fifteen years of his life building his empire from three small weaving cottages and now he had wealth and power.

'Morning, Mr Wild, sir.' The overseer of the mill was there to greet him at the end of Peat Street, the road that would lead to the gate of the mill.

'Everything well, Sampson?' Wild asked.

The man smiled up at him genially

from the nag he rode. 'Oh, yes, Mr Wild, working like clockwork.'

'Good man.' Oberon almost smiled back, but that would never do, it would be fraternising with the hired help; not at all advisable or proper. 'Mr Sampson, there is a Bible Moth in our midst.' Oberon paused long enough to stare into Sampson's beady eyes. He turned to Dermid, who had recovered his twisted smile.

'Is there, sir?' Sampson asked, with raised eyebrows.

'Yes. And I rely on you two gentlemen to see to it that he is persuaded to find his true light elsewhere, or realise his own may be shortly extinguished? There is neither need nor place for him here!'

'Yes, sir.' The men nodded, smiled knowingly, and bowed to their master.

Oberon looked at his horse's mane. 'Good, good.' It was a brilliant day today. He stroked the tall, black and handsome beast and Oberon thought it suited him well enough because he still had his good looks. He always walked tall, fasted on a Friday and ate his fill Saturday through till Thursday. It was what kept him, in his estimation, so humble.

Of course, he made sure his wife, Prudence, did nought to excess as that would be no good for a woman; a wife should be but modest and unspoiled. Knowing that females fought to control their emotions, it was better that a wife should not have hers aroused. She was neither gifted, nor intelligent or attractive in his more worldly experience.

He liked slender and lean women, but he needed heirs, lots of them hopefully, just in case the cholera broke out — at least four fine sons would do. So he had chosen a woman with childbearing hips, a plain countenance and a gentle non-demanding nature — oh, and of course a rich father. Prudence would do fine.

He glanced at the sky. No, he would return to his true love, the object of his earthly desire. Oberon reasoned that as he was a mere man, and a man of his standing had to have some sin to repent.

The black iron gates appeared through the smog as he came to the end of Peat Street, and he stopped and waited for the two liveried gatekeepers to open them wide for him to ride in. He nodded to Dermid to release him to do his 'other' chores.

He would not be needed until Mr Wild left the mill at his usual hour and was ready for his escort back through the streets to civilisation and safety beyond the old part of town.

This was his moment of joy. As people poured into the mill, bent and tattered, he rode by them. The best part of the day was complete and his mill noisily produced his wealth, securing his future and more importantly the future of his son. For this very morning his wife, Prudence, had told him that she was with child. After four long tedious months of wedlock, she had finally fulfilled her duty and now he could return to his lover.

He smiled. One day his son would ride in here with him. Oberon, despite his grim expression, was a decidedly happy man. He stopped in the middle of the road. The stream of workers drifted in through the narrow door to the left of the ornate gates and another stream looking weary filed out through the doorway to the right.

Some glowered at him as he sat upon his fine steed, dressed in his black hat, long coat and trousers.

'Ungrateful scum,' he chastised them as they dared to so much as look upon him with anything less than gratitude.

The two men who ran out to open the black iron gates waited patiently, so that he may ride in, as was his custom every morning bar Sunday. He finally cantered his horse into the stable area of the yard. The lad who awaited his arrival took the horse's reins and bowed.

He always arrived at the same time, always with the same curse to his fellow man. But one man, unseen in the crowd, glared out at him, and swore to himself, 'One day, man, I'll get yer, when no-one's lookin'.'

'Ned!' hush yer mouth man. Do yer want to be hung?' The voice of a passer-by whispered in his ear and pushed him on before he could be seen.

Ned walked but his heart was filled with grief and hatred. He would reap revenge on the brute of a man called Oberon Wild for the death of his beloved wife, Elizabeth. It might take him to the end of his days but he would — one day.

★   ★   ★

Prudence Wild felt her stomach gently and smiled as the child within moved, both strongly and constantly. A healthy boy, she was sure it was, and for that she would be grateful, as it would have to be strong to hold his own ground against her husband, Oberon.

She sighed in despair as she realised she was too gentle a character to make a stand against such a man. Prudence could see this, but that was her lot in life and she had accepted it with good grace. Gone were her dreams of a man she could love and respect, who would love her son, in return. She had little love and even less respect for the bully who ruled over her life.

How charming he had been when he had first courted, how naïve she had been, and now he made no attempt to hide the evil that lay within him. She hugged her stomach and sighed, a tear falling silently for her eye. 'Let it be a boy, dear God.' She prayed with all her heart because then he might leave her alone. Prudence decided she was going to change her character — somehow she had to.

She had been brought up to be submissive, to obey and was told that in return a husband would treat her with respect, love and gentleness. Like a fool she had believed every word her mama had spoken.

He would have to treat her with more

respect, surely. Her son would give her courage, and through him she had rediscovered a reason to live. She asked her merciful God that the child would be like her, gentle of temperament and loving in spirit and knew it would not be like the cold heart that belonged to her husband. This child would be hers.

2

'Mother, can I walk out in the snow? Please?' Nineteen-year-old Faith asked Prudence beseechingly. 'I could wear my old boots . . . please? I promise I'll take care and won't slip or succumb to a chill.'

'No. Absolutely not. You know your father doesn't approve of you doing things like that anymore. You're nearly nineteen, Faith, a bit old to be playing in the snow, dear. You are a young lady and should be learning how to become more like one . . . you're not a boy.' Prudence looked at her daughter with love in her eyes and Faith beamed knowingly back.

'I know, Mother, I'm not a boy! Father reminds me of it often enough. But he is in Edinburgh. Please let me . . . just this once . . . please?' Faith smiled beguilingly.

'You're a wicked young girl. You would have me in more trouble than enough.' Prudence sighed, shaking her head; her bonnet flopped from side to side as she moved. 'Slip out the servants' door and whatever you do, make sure no-one sees you from the road. Stay away from the iron gates! One hour, you hear me? One hour only. I don't want you to catch a chill.'

Faith kissed her mother's cheek and hugged her tightly. She loved her dearly and, besides, father was away. Life was peaceful — no more than that — perfect, because the snow had come. With any luck he would not return for days and then she would have her mother laughing and smiling with her as she always did when he was not there.

Faith hurried to dress up in her warmest and oldest clothes. Then she slipped out of the side of the house, crossing the grounds and disappearing into the trees at the edge of the estate. The air was icy and it clean took her breath away. She felt the cold prick the tender skin of her cheeks, and rubbed them with delight.

Faith felt free. If only every day could be like this one, happy. Her mother was so at peace when he was not there. The black silhouette of the trees against the white snow was beautiful, but as she walked farther towards the eastern wall the pure snow changed to a dirty grey. The trees had a layer of the same dirt colour upon them.

She climbed carefully up the fallen trunk of one tree that was propped at an angle against another. From the highest point she could see over the wall, but instead of the joy and happiness that had filled her spirits a few moments earlier, what she saw made her feel sad.

The large mill billowing away across the other end of the town had a permanent black cloud over it. The whole area looked sombre and some-what frightening to her. This was what her father had built. He boasted and bragged of his achievements, but Faith hated it. She wished she could stop the place, or at least modernise it. She had read in her father's news sheet about other mills and the changes and new thinking. There had also been articles of uprisings, machine wreckers.

Faith wondered if they would strike here. Each Sunday, in the old church, she saw the grim faces of the people who lived there and they scared her; old before their time. Only one appeared differently — the young man who always exchanged a look and a wink at her, unseen by her father, of course, or he would have him whipped raw for his insolence. But there was something about his impish face surrounded by his ash blonde hair, that made Faith feel warm and quivery inside.

Tomorrow was Sunday and if Father did not return she might be able to stay longer, as her mother liked to talk to the people, but Father would always insist they went straight back to the Hall in the carriage. He was like a prison guard.

She climbed precariously back down the trunk, returning to the house some two hours later.

'Faith Wild, I should lock you in your room for a week!' Her mother greeted her as she re-entered the house. 'I've asked Anna to pour a warm tub for you and a mug of hot chocolate. Go and warm yourself up, girl, this minute!'

'Thank you, Mother,' Faith said impishly. 'You're so thoughtful.' Faith giggled as Prudence shook her head at her, watching the girl run up the stairs two at a time.

'Walk with decorum, Faith.' Prudence laughed as Faith continued up with an exaggerated air, mimicking her father's habit of putting one hand in the small of his back as he walked.

Oberon Wild did not return that evening, as the snow had thickened upon the ground, so mother and daughter enjoyed a relaxed meal on a small table in the morning room. Both loved it as the view from the bay window looked over the estate and, with such a covering of snow, it looked marvellous.

The next morning the carriage was summoned so that they could go to church. Slowly and precariously it made its way through the town towards St Stephen's. Normally, it went at speed, not allowing the woman inside it to stare out at the mill workers or give time for them to stare back at Prudence and Faith.

Prudence sat back in the seat holding Faith's hand as her daughter eagerly watched the world that she rarely saw outside of her own home. It was an opportunity for her to expand her knowledge and as a bookish girl she found it fascinating, but it was not a sight she found at all comforting.

'If I owned this town I'd change things. You'd see what I'd do.' She looked back at her mother, her face set and determined.

'How would you do that?' Prudence asked with interest.

'I'd close down the mill,' she

answered calmly.

'Then how would the people survive?' her mother asked her.

'I would refit it, employ the workers to clean it and have work parties improving the conditions of their houses.' Faith peeped out of the window. 'I'd build one privy per two families.' Faith laughed as her mother's mouth dropped open in shock.

'What words to come out of your young mouth! How can you speak of such things?' Prudence shook her head.

'Why ever not? It is a natural part of life and their life lacks dignity.' Faith sat back and folded her arms in front of her, her view made, and her mind set.

'You shouldn't read your father's papers, Faith. He'd be furious if he knew. Have you been reading the letter from the new mill owners farther north, calling for change?' Prudence asked.

'How would you know that, Mother, unless you read the papers left on his desk too?'

Faith watched her mother's face

colour. 'Never mind, Mother. I will not say and neither will you. We shall both take extreme care not to be caught but how else are we to know what is going on?'

'Learn your needlepoint, pay attention to the finer things in life and please try to show you are making an effort to please your father.' Prudence looked at her daughter with such a serious expression that it made Faith smile slightly.

'You agree with me, though, don't you, Mother?' Faith saw a glimmer of humour cross her mother's eyes.

Prudence sighed and shrugged her shoulders, but Faith tapped her leg with her finger. 'Don't you?'

'Yes, but it is not our place to speak of such things. We must honour and respect your father, he . . . he is a good . . . he provides us with a good home.'

'Hmmm, but at what cost to them?' Faith blurted out her answer, and knew her words hurt her mother.

That was the last thing she wanted to

do, but there surely was a way they could still own the mill and live at Wildermill without such poverty existing in the town. She was not supposed to see or acknowledge it, but Faith found it impossible not to look and question.

Suddenly the coach lurched and both women were thrown forward into each other's arms. There was a loud crack sounding around them and it fell down at one side. They screamed involuntarily.

The horses neighed wildly in their harness and pulled, writhing until released from their burden and steadied by strong and determined hands.

Faith was the first to right herself from the melee. She held her mother firmly, making sure that she was not hurt in anyway.

'Whatever is the matter?' Prudence shouted to the driver as she too regained her composure.

'Sorry, ma'am. One of the horses slipped when the wheel gave way. We've damaged it I'm afraid. I'm going to have to ask you to step outside whilst we free the beast and have the wheel fixed.'

Faith quickly climbed outside and leaned back in to help Prudence. The driver excused himself and stepped in front of her, and she waited whilst her mother was helped out. The two women stared around them, wrapped as they were in long fine woollen coats carrying large fur muffs, their heads protected under beaver-lined bonnets.

'Please Mrs Wild, you really must come into the warmth. I am having a trap harnessed for you and you will be taken to the church shortly.' The owner of the blacksmith's, Josiah Baxter, was speaking to them and wearing his Sunday best.

Faith saw her mother smile broadly at him, and it made her feel a little odd because she never smiled so warmly at her father. 'Josiah, you are a guardian angel. Thank you for we are indeed two maids in distress.' Prudence's voice was light and good humoured, despite, Faith noticed, her rather nervous stance as she glanced at her surroundings.

'Then worry no more, but could I suggest that for your own safety we remove you from these streets as soon as possible?'

He raised an eyebrow and Faith looked around her to see a small crowd gathering. In the middle of them was a wild-looking man.

'Mrs Wild?' the man questioned, his voice slightly slurred. 'Is that chit of a wench really the gaffer's wife? Come to see how the 'rabble' lives, eh? Or have yer cum slummin' it to rub our noses in the muck you so proudly own?'

The man stepped forward and Faith stared at him. She had never seen such a look of hatred and loathing directed at her and her mother before. She cupped her mother's elbow, standing slightly forward from her in a protective manner.

'Ned, leave it. You're picking on innocent women . . . '

'Innocent! Innocent you say. It was more than the blood of animals that has been spilled to clothe those 'innocents' in fur.'

He stepped forward one pace, but two of Josiah's men blocked him. 'My wife died to pay for them!'

'Shut him up lads before he ends up in jail.' They took a step towards him whilst Josiah tried to direct Prudence and Faith out of the street and away from the fracas, but Faith pulled away.

'Please, leave him.' Her young voice brought silence to the gathering crowd.

The two men who had hooked an arm under each one of his, stared back at her in amazement as she spoke out in the stranger's defence.

'Faith, come with us now. This is no place for a young lady!' Prudence's voice was filled with anxiety.

'He is clearly unwell. Please take him home, safely . . . ' Faith looked at the two ruffians, but she was taken aback by the stark hatred in the eyes of the man called Ned.

A man broke through the crowd towards them. 'Josiah, pull back your men. I'll see to him. There's no need to cause him more pain than he inflicts upon himself.' The young man turned to his father and looked at him compassionately. 'Father, what have you been saying now?'

'Oh, the same that he has been saying those last nineteen years and it's amazing he hasn't been hung from the gallows tree for it!' Josiah's voice was harsh, but Faith noticed his face showed some sympathy at least for the young man.

Faith's blond admirer from the church had stepped between her and the three men.

'I think he is unwell. Would you take him home, please?' Faith looked up at the young man's face, filled as it was with concern for his father.

He saw Josiah's henchmen let go of his father, who collapsed in a heap on to the floor unable to support his own weight.

'I'm not unwell. They . . . ' The man tried to stand, but failed.

'I'll take him home, don't worry. I apologise, miss, that you had to witness this spectacle.' The man comforted and hushed his father.

'Do you not wish to apologise for what he said?' she asked quietly so that only he could hear her.

'No, miss, that I will never do.' His face was set and she was gripped by a stark reality that made her feel both shame and fear. As if he sensed her discomfort, he paused and smiled warmly at her. 'However, I am sorry that you should be tarnished by the shame your father alone should feel.'

His voice was equally low and honest. Faith could not help but let out a small gasp, shocked that he should speak to her in such a direct and personal way. 'I must bid you good day, Miss Wild.' He moved back a step and looked at Josiah as he helped his father to his feet.

'You do that, Benjamin, because if

Mr Wild hears of this there will be trouble for certain.' He looked at his men and said, 'Leave him, lads.'

'Thank you, Miss Wild,' Benjamin's words were said gently as he turned around and helped his father to stand. He pushed him firmly towards the gathered crowd who had supported the man's words and actions.

Faith nodded and was quickly taken on to the trap that had clattered up the road behind them, then on to the church.

Prudence was as white as a sheet. 'If your father hears of this it will not only be that man who suffers his wrath, Faith.'

Faith put her hand in her mother's who gripped it firmly. 'Tell me what the man meant. How did his wife die?'

Prudence shrugged her shoulders, not answering the question but stared silently at the church ahead of them as they approached the Norman building.

They were helped down by the priest who was most anxious that the two of them were welcomed correctly and escorted to their family pew without delay. Then he took up his usual position at the pulpit ready to sing the opening hymn.

Faith stared ahead of her, the man's bitter words still echoing in her mind . . . more than the blood of dumb animals . . . his wife had been killed, but how? She felt her cheeks burning. She looked down at the congregation gathered below and saw a raw poverty that was stark in its presence and condemnation of their own position and comfort.

She felt slightly sickly in her stomach. At once she recognised the overriding emotion within her. She really hated her father, and what a great sin that was, because it meant she could never honour him as the Bible demanded that she should.

3

Oberon arrived home later the following afternoon. Dinner had been prepared in case he should. The two women had recovered from the events of the previous day, and had just relaxed, believing that the head of the household had not made it through the snow-covered roads again.

They had started to talk about the village and Faith was waiting to broach the subject of the workers' housing. Their manner had lightened after an awkward start to the day so she was loathe to spoil the moment but she needed to know if there was anything she could do to help. Would father consider her organising charity from the wealthier houses on their side of town?

Ideas filled her head, from teaching the young children, to involving medical care of some sort. She had no worldly experience, but surely she could do something — if only her father could view it as a help to the mill and healthier and happier workers. The notion held great promise until she visualised her father, then it dispersed like the black clouds from the mill chimneys.

The door burst open banging against the plastered wall. An oil lamp wobbled upon a table, then steadied. Oberon had discarded his hat and coat, thrown at the doorman as he entered the house and proceeded at speed to the day room.

'Oberon . . . dear, sir. You have returned.' Prudence stood up, her manner flustered. The joy that had filled her face as mother and daughter sat looking at each other was gone. Faith felt a pain in her heart where happiness had been replaced by fear. 'I shall send for your meal straight-away.' Prudence walked away from her chair but before she had taken one step his voice bellowed out of his crimson cheeked face.

'You went out in the snow! You broke a wheel on the carriage, nearly crippled my horses and were nearly mauled by an angry mob in the street and you talk of dinner!'

Prudence stepped backwards feeling with her hand for the chair, as if his words had hit her with a physical blow.

'You make it sound so terrible; I should not exaggerate the situation . . . ' Prudence sat back down into the chair, as if she needed something solid behind her.

'You sit there, calmly, and tell me not to exaggerate! What would you have done if one of my fine horses had broken a leg?' Oberon's voice rose to an ever higher pitch. 'Or if our only child, Faith, my daughter had been . . . attacked or worse?'

Prudence braced herself for his next outburst and Faith sat, head bowed, in the corner of the room. She did not dare look up at him directly in case she betrayed her true feelings for him by disclosing a look of loathing in her eyes.

'It wasn't an 'angry mob', sir. I would describe it more of a group of curious people . . . ' Prudence's voice trailed off to a whisper as he leered at her as if she was utterly pathetic.

'Are you a complete ignoramus? Do you not know that mills have been burned to the ground or smashed to pieces by such rabble? They were spurred on by jealousy and greed. They see your finery woman and to them it is as a naked flame to an unlit prepared fire. They cannot control their avarice. It burns in their hearts and leaves their senses numbed to more Christian sensitivities. You not only risked your own life, woman, but that of my daughter. I had thought that even you would have had enough common sense to realise that!'

He shouted his last words accusingly at the slight figure of his wife. Oberon's substantial figure was dwarfing her, with his face no more than a foot away from hers. Faith wanted to scream at him, but she had to admit that she, too, feared his tempers.

Prudence did not reply at first, but Faith could see her mother's hand trembling on her lap from the corner of her eye.

'I would never endanger Faith's life. We were only going to church, sir,' Prudence protested pitifully.

'But you did! You did! Even now you fail to see the danger you were in.' Oberon leaned imposingly over his wife and she turned her face to the side staring out of the window. 'Your intelligence or lack of it amazes me, even now, at times like these.'

'Father, we were never in any danger. The blacksmith was there and his men. No-one threatened us . . . only offered us help.' Faith tried to sound confident as she spoke out, knowing that it would aggravate him even more, but unable to sit still and watch his tirade on her poor mother without offering her some kind of support in her defence.

After all, Faith realised that it was her

badgering that had worn down Prudence's resolve not to risk the journey. Faith had wanted to see the man she now knew was called Benjamin, again. She lifted her head slightly.

'Be silent, child! You are far too young and innocent to understand the ways of this world. This is why I have taken matters into my own hands.' Oberon strode over to his leather-covered chair by the fire. He lifted his pipe up from its rest on the mantelpiece and sat down with a contented look on his face.

Faith looked up directly at her father and saw her mother had done the same.

He seemed pleased to have attracted their undivided attention, as both females had been avoiding directly looking at him whilst he raged at them.

'What do you mean, Father?' Faith asked feeling an immediate sense of unease. What business had he gone to Edinburgh on, which could possibly concern her? No matter what she had done whilst he was away he must have made some kind of plans for her already. But what? He was merely using the coach incident as a justification for whatever it was he had been planning.

'Whilst in Edinburgh I made some enquiries amongst my colleagues and I have found the perfect match for you.' His sombre face broke into a rare and unkindly smile.

Faith stared wide-eyed at him as he smiled broadly back at her. She could see that he was very pleased with himself.

Faith and Prudence looked at each other, and daughter stood beside her mother holding tightly her trembling hand.

'What do you mean, Father? I have not yet come out or had a season,' Faith asked, although she had no wish to do so either. She was happy to stay with her mother . . . and be near Benjamin.

'No need for that. Parties are the feeding ground of Satan. You shall be married in the spring time and will then embark with your husband to your new home. It has all been agreed and I am well pleased with the arrangements.'

'Who is my husband to be, Father?' Faith asked, not believing the words that were coming from her lips. Flashes of the young man Benjamin crossed her mind, his rough good looks, the twinkle of mischief in his eye and the hatred of her mother in his father's. It was no good. He was socially of the wrong class and situation, but would her father choose for her such a fine young man as he? 'Have you found a young officer, Father?'

'What good would it do to wed you to a soldier? He could be dead before your first child was even born and then I'd have a young widow and his babe to marry off. No, he most certainly is not. He is the son of my good friend, Ambrose Stirling. His first wife died two years since of some fever or other, but he is ready to take on a second.

'He is rich, responsible and in need of fine strong heirs. Not old money but new money, like ours.' Oberon's accusing look at Prudence made her recoil further. 'If I have been cruelly denied a fine son of my own then I shall have a grandson to be proud of instead; in fact two; one to inherit their estates and one to inherit mine.'

'What do you mean . . . embark?' Prudence asked and stood unsteadily on her feet. One hand held her stomach and the other the back of the chair.

'He has bought a vast amount of land on which to breed his sheep. He will make it the largest estate in the colony within five years. I have seen his plans. They are splendid. Australia has a great future ahead of it and Sean will be in there from the start. Our two businesses will reunite to form one, an empire, and you, my dear Faith, will be the bond that joins the two families together. Do not let your Father down or your sons, because you will have them. You are young, strong and take after me. You, Faith, are Oberon's child, don't ever forget that and raise your head high with much pride.'

Prudence flopped back down in the chair again. Tears flowed as she clung to her daughter's hand once more.

'Father, I don't want to go to Australia. It's so far and . . . uncultured. I wouldn't know what to so.' Faith was at a loss for words.

'I expected tears and tantrums from your mother, Faith, selfish woman that she is. She would have you cosseted in her room to do her bidding and lose your life and future to her whim. But you, Faith, are strong like I am. You will go and obey your husband as is your sole purpose on this earth. You do not need to concern yourself with any other worry or matter than that. I have early reason to believe that you will succeed in that area where your mother has failed — abysmally.'

'Father, that is so cruel . . . ' Faith answered.

'The truth child often hurts, but we cannot shrink from it and expect it to go away. The cruelty in this marriage has been to me, no-one else. I expected heirs. She gave me one girl child and then became barren. A man of means bound to that!' He pointed at Prudence with his finger, a look of distaste on his face.

Prudence was now doubled up in misery and grief. Faith stroked her back, trying with all her might not to cry also.

Oberon walked boldly towards the door.

'Father, tell me something of the man I am to marry.' Faith swallowed, not wanting really to know, but desperate to think he might be remotely like Benjamin, at least in youth.

'I have told you as much about Sean Stirling as is important to know. The rest you will find out over many years of marriage.' He put his hand on the door handle and turned it.

'How old is he, Father?' Faith asked hopefully.

Oberon sighed, 'That is of no importance.'

'It is to me . . . Father. I am to be his wife.'

'You are blessed with a man of substance and experience. He is thirty-six and fit as a man ten years younger. You will make him very happy.' Oberon slammed the door shut behind him.

'Oberon's child,' Faith repeated the words with pure venom in her voice. The very term made her want to denounce him and his rotten empire. 'I hate him, Mother.' Faith said quietly but with absolution of truth.

Prudence sat up, breathing heavily and looked at her daughter through bloodshot eyes. 'I know, dear. God help me, I do too.'

'What are we to do, Mother? I cannot go to the other side of the world without you. I won't do it. If his view of you is so poor, then you could come too.' Faith looked at her mother full of renewed hope.

Prudence smiled, her tears stopped as she cupped her daughter's face in her hand. 'I would go with you to the ends of the earth if it were possible. I have no wish to see you caged or trapped in this hell with me. You have a right to live girl. But can't you see he would never allow me to go.'

'Why ever not? You heard the things he said. Why stay with such a man when he loathes you so?'

'Because he is a bully, child. He gains his strength at the expense of my weakness.'

Faith knew there was an unpalatable truth in what she heard. 'Then what can we do for I shall not marry a man I do not love, nor shall I leave you?'

'No, you shall not enter a loveless marriage. That I would not wish on any young girl. You might have to travel somewhere without me, though. I have no answers at the moment. This is all come as too much of a shock, but I give you my word, Faith, he will not ruin your life as he has mine. I cannot stand up to him, but I have spent years manoeuvring around him. Carry on as if you will be a dutiful daughter and give me time to think.'

Faith was surprised at her mother's words and the confidence they held within them. She seemed to have had a strange calm come upon her.

'And Faith, be careful of handsome young men who wink at pretty young girls in God's house, no matter how discreetly.'

Faith blushed as she realised just how astute her mother really was. She may appear to be scared of Oberon's shadow, but she was aware of everything she saw from behind it.

Faith blushed, 'Sorry, Mother. I'm sure he did not mean any disrespect. I didn't intend to encourage him.' Then a frightful thought crossed her mind. 'Did Father see him?'

'No, of course not, or he would have been chased around the town by your father's thugs. I try and keep you out of trouble and have done all my life, but there is only so much I can do. Take care, my dear. He must never suspect we could plan an escape from this hell he has created for us. Our only weapon is our intelligence because he credits us with absolutely none.'

'Mother, do you think we shall escape his plans . . . do we stand any chance when he is so powerful?' Faith asked, and saw a nervous smile cross Prudence's face. It grew and her mother's demeanour changed as she smiled broadly back at her.

'Yes, my dear. I do, without doubt, although it will not come easily, or cheaply, but I believe your father has just crossed a very fine, but important line.' Prudence patted Faith's hand gently.

'What line is that, Mother?' Faith asked impatiently.

'Mine, dear, mine.'

4

The next morning Oberon went out early to spend all day visiting his mills. He needed to re-establish his authority in case the men had lapsed in their duties during his absence.

Faith waited patiently for her mother to appear from her room, dressed and ready to go to town. She had been vague when they had broken their fast as to what it was they were to do this day so she sat quietly until they could safely take the carriage into the town to visit the milliner's shop.

They were also to call on Mrs Alexander Kilburn, wife of the Major, who oversaw the militia. Faith hated these visits as they invariably ended up with Mrs Kilburn relating all the local gossip in great detail to them whether they were interested or not, which her mother listened to with apparent joy;

that always surprised Faith as Prudence was far from a natural gossip.

Prudence alighted from the coach first, outside a small shop with a multi-paned window, Madame Fleur purveyors of fine clothing; it was a bay-fronted modern shop, with delicate little panels of glass, in the new part of town. Madame Fleur claimed that she provided the local gentry with their attire and was building up quite a reputation for elegance and taste.

However, most of their friends still went into Harrogate or York, so Faith was surprised that her mother had chosen this relatively unknown seam-stress to attend their needs.

'Ah, good day, Mrs Wild. We are honoured to have your company today.' Madame Fleur eagerly greeted her. Faith looked on at the sycophantic gestures and comments as she fawned over her mother like a bee to a sweet flower laden with nectar. She did no doubt smell the sweet scent of money, Faith mused. 'What can we provide our fine ladies with today? We have the latest design in Spencers which, as we speak, are gracing the carriages in St James Park itself in London.'

'I am surprised they fit them,' her mother said dryly, but her wit was lost on the lady who merely looked puzzled. 'I need to see your designs for wedding gowns. However, my daughter will need attire suitable for a warmer climate as well as winter garments and travel clothes for a long journey.

'In short, Madame Fleur she will need dressing from scratch, top to toe, for all seasons and in all situations. I will have nothing, but the very best made of the finest quality and in your most recent designs. My order will take at least three months to fill and I will not accept anything which is substandard or old in style.' Prudence looked at the woman whose eyes were locked in a moment of disbelief at her good fortune.

Faith almost laughed out loud as the woman could obviously not believe what she had just heard.

'I can assure you we only provide the very best, par excellence. Nothing less will do for my customers.' Then with a clap of her hands all was a blur of activity. Refreshments were sent for. The best tea was provided, in the finest china tea service on a silver tray.

Once they had partaken of their repast Faith was whisked away and her measurements were recorded in detail. Prudence rejected one fine cloth after another until she had the very best of everything. Patterns were agreed, prices fixed and dates arranged for the fittings.

Faith watched and listened transfixed by the calm and confident way her mother handled the whole business. What was her mother up to? Surely her father would faint at the cost of it all. Yes, Prudence was in her element. Faith noticed that amongst the finery and the pretty frippery were some very basic riding outfits; one for her and one for Prudence.

She had also included a few essentials for herself. Her mother was, she decided, creating a huge smoke screen and plotting their escape, but she risked a great deal because her father was a man who knew little compassion and no mercy.

Two-and-a-half hours later the women returned to their carriage.

'Mother, have you lost your senses? Father will be irate . . . ' Faith saw a glint in Prudence's eyes.

'Your father will have to accept that preparing a daughter for her wedding and emigration to a strange land will cost him . . . dearly. You will need things that you cannot possibly buy there. You shall have the best, and he will pay for it, of that I will make sure, most dearly!' Prudence snapped her words out bitterly.

'But, Mother, I thought we are planning . . . you know, are we not?' Faith looked at her mother and saw she possessed a strange confidence about her.

'Yes, dear we are. For I shall now do what I have not dared to more than dream about these last nineteen years, but he has now provided me with the means and the motive to carry it through.'

'Tell me what it is, please?' Faith almost begged, but her mother shook her head.

'You, for your part, are the young excited betrothed. Enjoy all the fuss and leave the plotting to me. We have to be patient, but you will not be travelling from these shores on your own. That I promise you.'

'I don't want a husband, Mother!' Faith replied, as the coach made its way up the driveway towards the home of Major Kilburn.

'Dear child, you would if he was the right man for you.' Prudence smiled at her daughter and Faith's heart felt suddenly full of grief for the lost love of her mother. Such a fine woman should not have had to survive years of abuse at the hands of a heartless bully such as her father.

The coach slowed to a halt and the footman unfolded the steps so that the ladies could alight and climb the grand stairs to the entrance of the hall.

'Why did we have to come here, Mother? I thought you loathed the woman,' Faith whispered into her mother's ear.

'Why dear, yes, you do look a little pale!' Prudence explained as she stared at Faith.

Faith wondered if her mother had misheard her or gone quite mad. Perhaps it was all becoming too much for her.

'Benjamin, be so good as to escort Miss Wild back to Wildermill Hall and return for me in two hours.' Prudence spoke sternly to the new footman who Faith had paid very little attention to.

'Yes, ma'am.' The young man bowed in his liveryman's uniform and turned to Faith offering her his arm as she climbed back into the coach. As she sat back on the seat her face was not more than a few inches from the familiar blue eyes and blond hair of the young man who was folding up the step behind her, before closing the carriage door.

He winked at her mischievously as she saw to her amazement beyond the uniform to the face who so often sought her out in the church. It was he, her Benjamin. Prudence waved to her from the top step and Faith could see the satisfaction in her mother's eyes. Surely she was not match-making her to a footman? Her father would have a fit. Faith sat back and smiled at the thought which, to her, was quite comforting.

5

'Obee, my sweetest darling. I'm so excited that I just cannot tell you how much! Your generosity overwhelms me.' Madame Fleur had entered his office on the top floor of the mill. She came there every Wednesday at precisely one o'clock. Fleur arrived, as always by his enclosed staircase on the outside of the building and unseen by the mill workers.

She locked the door behind her and then the one that led to the factory offices. Knowing, that failing a major incident in the mill itself, they would not be disturbed.

'Then don't waste your words trying, woman, show me instead.' Oberon Wild swivelled his chair away from the desk so that he could see his visitor without obstruction. His lips curled upwards in the right-hand corner; this was his smile.

'Indeed, you are the most generous man in the whole of the north of England. Of that I am sure!' Madame Fleur massaged his head with the tips of her fingers in slow circular movements. She leaned forwards and his eyes sparkled with anticipation. No perfume or finery had been spared for him on this visit, not after he had sent his poor excuse for a wife to her, instead of the larger and older milliners in the next established town of Harrogate.

She had decided to employ an extra seamstress just to focus on his order. It would be the talk of the town and that guaranteed that her name would go hand in hand with it. Soon her name would be spoken of in York, Harrogate and then, in time, even in London itself, for she was a lady of ambition.

'And you, my little Rose, are true to your name, all scent and soft petals, or perhaps the prickliest barb a man can become hooked upon.'

'So what is it you want from me today, my love?' He gripped her firmly and she shivered involuntarily. It was what he paid her for. It was why they were a perfect match. For he knew she had the knowledge of her past existence gained in the high-class boudoir of the city.

In exchange he had given her respectability and a business life of her own. She hated him and even if he sensed it, he did not care because he loved what she could do for him, and did willingly so long as he kept her out of the brothel in which he had found her.

'Why, no more than you have already done. For I shall promise you your daughter will look fit to marry a prince, Obee.' She looked down on his balding head with her usual distaste.

'What do you mean?' His tone was harsh. He gripped her narrow waist with such pressure that this time she was in real pain.

'Your wife of course . . . she has

placed an order for your daughter's trousseau with me ... Surely you knew?'

He lifted her from his lap, then tossed her light body away from him until, half naked, she landed on his office floor. 'Dress, woman. I shall return to you tonight when I am ready. Make, sure you are!'

He unlocked the door, leaving her groping for her clothes on the floor, the very garments which he had so eagerly removed from her only moments before, and marched out.

She slammed the door shut behind him before his clerk could see her and hastily she re-dressed. Madame Fleur was seething. She was not about to be thrown away by such a loutish brute. Once she had made her name and money she would move her establishment to a more fashionable part of the country and find herself a real gentleman. Until then, though, she would have to prepare herself for him tonight, she would have her brandy ready to drink for when he finally slept, to numb her senses.

Faith felt the coach slow down. She gripped the canary yellow upholstered seat as the vehicle turned off the main roadway. It stopped at the side of a quiet track far beyond the town and the Major's house. The footman's familiar face appeared at the door to the carriage.

'Ma'am, are you still feeling ill?' he asked nervously. 'Would you like to take some air, a gentle walk with me, perhaps?' Benjamin raised an eyebrow as he smiled hopefully at her.

Faith looked out of the window and saw that they were on a little-used track in the wooded vale. He stepped away from the carriage door as if to show her that he meant her no harm.

'You are perfectly safe, Miss Wild. I am here with your mother's blessing. I wanted to talk to you alone . . . that is all.'

Faith opened the door herself and he came swiftly forward to offer her his arm as she alighted from the vehicle. The ground was still firm with frost so she placed her booted foot carefully upon the rock hard ground.

'This is highly irregular!' Faith snapped, more fearful of what her father would say if he found them together in such a remote spot, than of the young man in whose company she was.

'Perhaps so, but how else were we ever to speak to each other, openly?' Benjamin smiled at her, still with a slightly tense appearance.

'Why should we talk to each other openly or otherwise, sir? You are quite presumptuous,' she exclaimed slightly haughtily, and looked away from him.

'Why indeed!' he mocked her manner then laughed openly, and the cheeky face who had caught her eye in church returned to him, confident and relaxed.

She blushed slightly. 'What is it you wish to say?' Faith asked, as she walked away from the carriage and looked up at the beauty of the undisturbed nature around her. Her fur bonnet and muff were much needed against the frosty bite to the air.

'I wanted to say,' he paused by her and looked deeply into her eyes.

Faith could not help admire the handsome broad shoulders of this man. He could not look more desirable to her if he wore the green jacket of the fighting elite in the army. She tilted her head on one side as she listened to his words, and as she returned his intimate stare he continued, 'That you are the most naturally beautiful young woman I have ever seen and I apologise for the insults that my father hurled at you and your mother in the street two weeks ago. I would not have had him shamed or you publicly ridiculed for the entire world to see, if I could have only prevented the situation from arising. I could not apologise then, but I do so now.'

His smile had gone and, with their eyes still drawn to each other, she listened to the sincerity of his words and manner. The compliment within them was not lost on her either.

'I thank you for your apology and for the flattery that you bestow upon me. But, tell me why you are not like them? Why are you here? Why would my mother risk my reputation to a mere stranger?' Faith watched as he looked down, almost shame-faced. A lock of his blond hair hung across his forehead and Faith had to control an urge to flick it out of the way with her finger.

'I am 'like' them, Miss Wild. I was born one of them. However, the reverend's wife, my aunt, was broken-hearted when my mother died and she graciously took me in. I have had a full education, which places me apart from my own 'kind'. I can read, write, paint, ride and understand how to work the land, or I should manage the land, but have no place in your society. I am an outcast of both.' He still stared directly at her, and she at him.

'Then what is to be done with you?' Faith asked.

'That is up to you, Miss Wild. You are in a precarious position and I do not envy you. Do as your father wishes and you risk a hard life of loveless toil, or . . . ' He sat on a tree stump beside her.

'You are remarkably well informed, sir.' Faith saw humour cross his dark brown eyes. 'Or, what?'

'Or consider an alternative, that would free yourself, your mother and myself in one daring go. However, it would be dangerous and requires a great deal of secrecy and trust between the three of us, for if one falls down then we all do.' He gently held her hand.

She felt the warmth of his flesh against her and her heart quickened.

'Does Mother know you are talking to me of this?' Faith asked.

'Yes, it is she who has spoken to me. I should never have dared to approach you with such an outrageous idea if I had not had the good fortune to be approached firstly by Mrs Wild.' He was looking at her with such warmth and conviction that his eyes almost glistened as the autumnal sun glinted off them.

'I do not understand what it is that you imply. What of your Father?' Faith was surprised when he pulled his hand away and lowered his head.

'You were not told?'

Faith bent down so as to see his face clearly once more. They were filled with sadness. 'Told what?' she asked.

'He fell into the river. Two days after your coach broke down in town. He was drunk as usual. He lived and died a bitter man.' Benjamin stood upright.

'What of your family?' Faith watched as he stared at her.

'Miss, my mother died, so did my baby sister. There was no other family after that, save my aunt and uncle.' He ran his fingers through his hair. 'This is folly, you are a lady and your father is a powerful man. I have no right to interfere in your life, ruin your reputation and your future, for you at least have one.'

'You do too, if I say you have, so waste no more time. Tell me what is it you and Mother have in mind?'

* * *

Oberon stormed through the office, down the main staircase and out into the yard. 'Saddle my horse, immediately!' The stable hand ran as fast as he could to fetch his master's mount. 'Where is Dermid? Fetch him!' Oberon shouted as he paced impatiently up and down the flagstones as he waited for his horse.

The liveried doorman ran into the street, crossing the cobbles and into the Pestle and Mortar. It was where Dermid always awaited his master's call.

Within moments the man returned with Dermid and his rifle in tow. The man was sent straight into the stable nearly knocking the young lad over as he emerged with Oberon's horse, ready to go.

Wild climbed on to his mounting block and straddled the animal. He had his crop at the ready. 'Dermid! Dermid! You lazy Irish . . . '

Dermid rode out of the stables, stopping alongside Wild. He stared at him blankly, but Oberon saw the hatred in his eyes, as a twitch betrayed the man's loathing of anyone who poured disdain on his ancestry.

'And about time too. I don't pay you to sup ale all day long. Now, escort me. I wish to return home.'

Oberon kicked his horse on and galloped through the mill gates nearly knocking a man off his feet. Dermid followed not questioning his master's unusual break with routine, particularly on a Wednesday lunchtime because Dermid knew Oberon's arrangement, for it was he who escorted the 'lady' in and out of the grounds unseen.

Once through the mill town and on to the open road, Wild headed straight for Wildermill Hall, only to find that his wife had taken herself off to the Major's house for the afternoon and was not expected to return until shortly before his own arrival. Wild was irate.

He had wanted Prudence to be enthusiastic about her daughter's marriage, reluctantly no doubt but, to take such matters into her own hands without discussing a budget or anything with him was intolerable. Then there was the other issue. The stupid woman had taken his innocent daughter, Faith, to the establishment of a common harlot — his harlot.

The woman had no taste but it showed she had even less sense. She wasn't to know who she was dealing with. Prudence was too naïve to figure that out he admitted to himself, but if this order went through he would be paying his wench twice over and a tidy sum at that. It would be stopped. Oberon would take control again. It had never before been anything other than his.

He arrived to find that Prudence was not there — she was not where he wanted her. His temper rose to its peak. He threw a vase across the hallway and ordered that it be cleaned up immediately then mounted his horse and galloped off down the drive once more.

Faith listened to Benjamin's words in disbelief. 'Australia!' she looked away. 'But that is where my father intends to send me anyway. They have contacts there. Surely we would be found out.'

Benjamin placed her hand in his.

'Not if you had a different name and were travelling with your husband and his mother.' He squeezed her hand gently in his. Her face flushed as she stared at him, her mouth dropping open. She appeared to be stunned by his words, and she slowly pulled her hand from his. 'Are you proposing to marry me, Benjamin?'

He turned around and took two strides away from her before stepping up on to the fallen tree trunk. He looked back at her, his arms out-stretched in an apologetic gesture. 'You don't need to embarrass or distress yourself on my account. The situation is hopeless. I see that. I was a fool to believe it would be any other way between us.

'I apologise for having the nerve to even suggest the idea. I assure you that if your mother, a lady I hold in the highest esteem, had not given me permission to speak to you in such a personal fashion, I should never have dared to.' His arms dropped to his sides as he stepped dejectedly back down on to the forests leafy ground.

Faith paused for a moment then returned to the carriage. She opened the door without speaking, feeling his presence closing on her before he spoke.

'I'm sorry, Miss Wild. Please forget my words. I should never have approached you directly on such a matter.' He placed a hand upon hers as she held the door handle.

Faith turned around, her body almost touching his. She saw the sadness in his eyes and the disappoint-ment on his face. 'I need time to think this over, Benjamin.' She brought a gloved finger up to his lips to silence him, and stilt his reply. 'Let me consider your proposal seriously and talk to my mother. She must have a clear plan in mind. You have neither distressed nor embarrassed me. I am most flattered you would consider me suitable after what has passed between my family and yours.'

He brought his head close to hers and she allowed her instincts to override her sense of propriety, raising his lips to his. Their mouths touched lightly at first, his arms encircled her, drawing her close to him in an intimate embrace. Faith could feel the urgency in his caress as the passion between them increased.

It was only the sound of a galloping horse travelling along the road beyond the cover of the trees that caused them to part. Benjamin ran to a clearing in the trees to see who had ridden by in such urgency. Faith breathed in deeply. She tasted her lips then covered them in a guilty manner with her gloved hand. Never had her senses felt so alive, so strange, yet the desire within her was real and strong.

Benjamin returned to her with a flustered expression that told her their moment of privacy and intimacy had passed them by. It was necessary for them to return to their true stations in life.

She climbed inside the carriage as he arrived to hold the door open for her.

'Who was it?' Faith asked him, her own cheeks still red with her residual emotions. With confusion blurring her senses, she felt strange. Something inside her had awoken and somehow her life would never be the same again.

'It was your father, Faith. He must know something is amiss as he never leaves the mill at this hour. We must return quickly to collect your mother, because if he finds us here I fear you would be locked away within that gilded cage of yours until the day you are wed.

'He has found a man for you, Faith. Oberon Wild is a man who does not take kindly to being crossed; he likes to get his own way.'

He cupped her cheek in one of his strong hands. 'And the thought of you being out of my reach forever is, more than, I could bear . . . not now I know how you truly feel about me.'

Faith smiled. 'What we both feel may be of little import to my father. However, my mother holds the key to our future happiness; if we are to have one, that is.'

He closed the door and with haste they returned to the road, travelling towards the major's house. The coach pulled up outside the grand doors and they waited patiently until Prudence was escorted down the grand stairs. Benjamin helped her inside the coach and Faith sat quietly within the shadows unseen by the household staff.

The coach pulled steadily away. 'Did you enjoy your visit, Mother?' Faith asked.

'No, but then I never do. However, it is amazing what that lady knows about matters that I would have no knowledge of, left to your father's will.'

'Did you enjoy your visitor?' Her mother watched her face closely as if judging her reactions and intimate thoughts.

'Mother, why did you not warn me? He could have been most improper and what would I have done?' Faith could feel her face flushing despite her attempt to handle the question calmly.

'What would you have liked to have done 'if' he had, Faith?' Prudence stared at her intently.

'Mother!' Faith snapped at her a little too defensively.

'Faith, if I hadn't absolute trust in Benjamin I should never have allowed him to see you on his own. Or do you think I am as careless with your welfare as your father thinks I am?' Prudence did not smile and Faith instantly felt sorry that she had spoken in such a high-handed way.

'No, of course not.' Faith leaned forward and held her mother's hand.

'Then answer me honestly, Faith, because if you have feelings — strong feelings for him I will give you my blessing and will see to it that your trousseau is not wasted.'

Faith smiled broadly at her mother. 'I can't explain it. I have never really spoken to him before, yet we have watched each other grow, from afar, with an unspoken bond between us for years. But how can I marry a man without father's knowledge and blessing?'

'It will be arranged when the time is right. All I need to know at this juncture is that you would find happiness with Benjamin, the rest will fall into place. Be patient and trust me, Faith. Do nothing unusual and keep calm.'

Faith hugged her mother; the moment would have been perfect if not for one huge obstacle — her father.

6

'Ma'am, there's a messenger waitin' for you out the back.' The young attendant nervously interrupted her mistress, and added a little curtsy as an afterthought when Mrs Bickerstaff gave her a stiff look.

'Then he will have to wait, Millie. I am busy at the present time. Can you not see that, girl?' Madame Fleur smiled at the doctor's wife, Mrs Bickerstaff, as she showed her latest patterns to her. 'They are freshly arrived from London, Ma'am,' or so she told the woman, who had little sense of fashion.

'Pardon, Madame, but I fear it is most urgent.' Millie's voice was a little shaky and Fleur realised that it must be a messenger from Wild, or the girl would never have dared to interrupt her.

She was far from happy to discover that it was Dermid who stood waiting for her with his rifle at his side. She stared at him with loathing, partly because they understood each other only too well. They had both started life on the wrong side of a town and now served the same master. 'Now?' she asked.

'Now,' he answered smugly.

Fleur let out a long sigh. 'This will not do,' she muttered to herself.

The large Irish man curled one side of his mouth into what appeared to be a grin. 'Will you tell him that, or should I?'

She glared at him. 'I'll be one minute. Wait here.' She turned swiftly and left to fetch her cloak. How would he expect her to leave her customer's fitting with no notice and attend to him, her unexpected visitor? It was highly unprofessional and she had to lie appallingly to save her face in front of Mrs Bickerstaff.

Also she had no choice but to

promise an extra little something for her client, because of her unexpected departure. It would cost her, but Fleur would keep her clientele sweet — and she in turn had to oblige her benefactor.

Oberon had arrived at their private room and had sent Dermid to fetch her. It was very embarrassing to be at his beck and call. They had an agreement and he was not adhering to it. She did not want to have open ridicule or gossip about her in the town for that would destroy all she had worked to achieve — respectability.

However, Mrs Bickerstaff's order was nothing in comparison to the business that Mrs Wild had given her that very morning. So to keep the order that her business so desperately needed, she had no choice but to attend to Oberon's wishes. The thought made her shiver; he must be in a foul mood to come for her mid afternoon.

He had left his beloved mill. She in turn was developing a liking for her own free will and a little luxury, something that had been all too new to her until recent years. One day she would be free of him and all of his kind, but unfortunately not yet.

She wrapped her cloak around her body, feeling the smooth silk lining with her hands as she fastened the ornate enamel clasp at her neck. She had never forgotten the rough fabric of the gowns she had grown up in — coarse woollen dresses, which she would grow out of before the poorhouse staff replaced them, and her feet would be left bare when one pair of shoes fell apart and another cast-off pair had not arrived in her size from the charity of the town.

Her life had improved a thousand-fold since then, which was why she would do what she must to protect her present position and her future.

She crossed over from the back street where the man Dermid waited for her to escort her to the private room that Oberon paid for. It was in the back of an old inn.

Inside the sumptuously-decorated room, with its Romanesque style drapes and furnishings, it was just like the place in which he had first met her. Fleur was well aware that it was his way of letting her know precisely where she truly belonged.

Madame Fleur took a deep breath as they approached the door. Dermid's lip curled. She saw it, but did not look directly at him. He was as much Oberon's puppet as she was.

'Obee, you are early, my love. I did not expect you back so soon or I should have been ready for you.' She sensed his anger as she slipped inside the room. He did not even speak to her, just stood there in the middle of the rug, fully-clothed, waiting impatiently for her to arrive.

She released her cloak and hung it carefully on the hook on the wall.

'Would you like a drink . . . your favourite perhaps?' she gestured to the decanter and crystal glasses that were always kept full and ready for him on the small bedside table, but he merely shook his head. This was not a good sign. She smiled at him, walking up to him slowly and sensuously. She stroked his cheek tenderly with her fingers. He held them firmly in his hand, then, he bent her arm back behind her still keeping her within his grip.

'My daughter is a lady of refinement. She has no business being in your presence — or should I say, you in hers. You should not be attiring her, corrupting her innocence!' His words were spoken with bitterness and hatred.

'But Obee, your wife she came to me. I did not know they were to arrive. They had no appointment. I presumed you had sent them . . . Obee, ow my arm, it hurts!'

'Yes, you presume, madam, too much. I shall see that you do not do so again!'

'Obee!'

★   ★   ★

Prudence and Faith returned home to find the housekeeper was most upset by Mr Wild's earlier outburst. She was sent to her room and Mrs Bull, the cook, was told to send her a warm drink of milk and honey to calm the woman's nerves. Prudence did not want to have to replace her at this particular time. The fewer strangers around them the better if everything was to appear normal.

'Mother, what are we to do?' Faith asked anxiously.

'Nothing, my dear.' Her mother patted her back and returned to the day room where a warm fire glowed in the hearth.

'How can you say that? He is in one of his blind furies. We have spent far too much.' Faith paced up and down the room but her mother sat quite still.

'No, we have not. I doubt it is the reason that he is so upset.' Prudence flushed slightly.

'I do not understand, Mama. What other reason could there possibly be?'

Faith saw a flicker in her mother's eye of something more powerful than mischief, but Faith did not understand what it was.

'Just trust me, Faith, and ride the storm. For I suspect a whirlwind is about to arrive in our house.' She smiled at her daughter. 'Be calm yourself, but show your excitement about all the lovely things we have ordered. It is your trousseau. I want you to tell him all about it and how nice Madam Fleur was to you.'

'If you are certain,' Faith replied, taking comfort from her mother's surety. 'But what of Benjamin? Does he know he is working here now?'

Prudence's demeanour changed in an instant. 'You must not give him a second look or thought. Do not mention him. I shall arrange a suitable opportunity for you to meet him again for I want you both to be certain of your feelings for each other. Do not try to see him yourself. I'm serious Faith — this is no game we play. Your father has not paid any attention to his employment here so we shall not bring it to his attention.

'I suggested we had a chaperone at all times because of the political climate at present concerning mill owners.' Prudence jumped as the hall's main door was opened and Oberon returned.

Faith sat down on the window seat and picked up her embroidery. When her father appeared in the doorway, Faith looked up to greet him. Her face was all animation as she told him with great enthusiasm of the order that had been placed with Madam Fleur's establishment.

'Calm yourself, my dear child. I am delighted that you find the experience so gratifying.' He placed a hand on his daughter's shoulders to steady her, and smiled genuinely upon her innocent face. 'Which is why I am so pleased that you will have the thrill of going through the whole experience again in an establishment more befitting your position.'

'Again?' both women exclaimed at the same time. Prudence stood up. Faith realised that this was not a part of her mother's plan and she wondered what they were to do now.

'Yes, I'm afraid to have to tell you that Madam Fleur was set upon this afternoon by some lout . . . such times we live in. She has had to close up her shop for a short while and cancel her new orders and will not be able to fulfil yours. I shall arrange for you to go into Harrogate the day after tomorrow. Nothing will be spared, you shall have a fine trousseau made by a house of more 'refinement'.'

Oberon stared at Prudence. 'You really should have consulted me first, woman. One day you will learn to pay your due respect to your husband. Now, you must excuse me whilst I wash and change for dinner, then you can tell me all about the choices you have made, and I shall guide you as to their suitability, where your mother has failed.'

'What of Madam Fleur, is she badly hurt?' Faith asked.

'Nothing broken, but she is quite shaken by the experience.' Oberon walked calmly to the door to leave them.

'Who did it, Father?' Faith watched his expression closely. He shrugged his shoulders.

'No-one has been found, but I'm sure that the perpetrator is far away by now. I've set my man Dermid to find out if he is still in town.' He left the room and Faith stared at Prudence who had gone more than a little pale.

'Mother, you should not take his words to heart so. He always puts you down, but I know it is he who is the brute.' Faith watched her mother's face. 'But that poor woman. I hope they bring the man concerned to justice.'

'Yes, Faith, he is a brute. Even more of one than even I had judged him to be. Tomorrow I must go out early. You stay in your bed and sleep on. I will be back by mid-morning, and Faith, be careful, you must stay in your room until I return. Now, let us prepare for dinner.' Prudence left, but went to the servants' passage and not up the stairs to her room.

Faith thought about following her but thought she should make sure her father did not return before her mother, or else she would be in for another lecture about her place and ignorance.

Faith wondered who she needed to see in such a rush and why she should be going out early in the morning. There would be only one way to find out and Faith intended to be there too.

When Oberon left the following morning Prudence arrived in her riding attire. She made her way to the stables. Benjamin greeted her.

'Ma'am, are you sure you want to do this? I mean, the danger to yourself could outweigh any benefit your visit may offer you.' Benjamin mounted a horse also.

'I am quite sure. You are a good boy, Ben, however, this is one visit that is some years overdue.' Prudence was about to ride out into the yard when Faith appeared in the doorway.

'Then let us all go together, Mother. We appear to be a party to something underhand anyway.'

'Faith, you must stay here. This is a fool's errand,' Benjamin turned to Prudence, 'If you don't mind my saying so and I don't want you hurt.' Benjamin surprised both women, but it was to Faith's amazement that her mother sided with him.

'You must stay here. Your father would be angry enough if he discovers I have done this, but if you were seen I should be the subject of all his vitriol.'

'Perhaps, we all will be. Tell me where you are going, why? And when you intend to return, then I may consider your request, otherwise I shall follow you both!' Faith folded her arms and stared at them.

Benjamin's face betrayed his annoyance at her, whilst her mother gritted her teeth as she mulled over what to do about her headstrong daughter.

'Come and ride through the woods with us. We shall talk there, then, we shall see if you should return.' Prudence looked at Benjamin who was about to speak out. She raised her hand to him. 'This is a bad enough matter any way you look at it. Let us not make it worse.' She rode on and mother and daughter left Wildermill Hall together with their escort following a few feet behind them.

Faith smiled back at him, but his face was set. He was worried about her and although she did not care for him to tell her what she should or should not do she found it had a strange effect on her. Faith realised she quite liked it, oddly enough.

7

Faith and her mother entered the cover of the woods. 'Mother, please tell me who it is you are going to visit and why?' Faith watched Prudence closely. Daily she seemed to be showing more confidence. It was the threat to Faith's happiness that had given her courage to take control of her own life.

'It will be Madame Fleur that we see, if she can get away unnoticed.' Prudence stopped and waited for Benjamin to catch up with them.

'Why? Are you and she friends? I didn't realise that you were already acquainted.' Faith saw Prudence put her head back and laugh. It was an unusual yet pleasing sight as it was so natural, honest and free.

'No, Faith, but we have had something in common for many years.' She looked at Benjamin who nodded knowingly. 'She has been your father's mistress for quite some time I believe.'

Faith could hardly believe her ears. Her own father had a mistress. The thought was quite unpalatable to her. 'I don't understand. How could he?'

'Faith, you are still very naïve. I should not be discussing this with anyone, especially you.' Prudence smiled at her apologetically.

'No, Mother, you misunderstand me. I do not mean that I am shocked that a man has a mistress, rather I am amazed that a lady such as Madame Fleur would have a man as . . . as rough in manner and as opinionated as Father.'

Prudence shook her head, and Benjamin laughed. 'It is not as it appears. I have it on good authority that she was a woman of the night who he brought back with him from one of his trips to London.

There was a time when he visited the city regularly. However, once Madame Fleur arrived here his visits to the city almost stopped. It did not take a genius to figure out why. I am only amazed that the whole town is not awash with gossip of it.'

'Oh Mother, he has been an absolute beast to you, truly horrible!' Faith snapped the words out. 'If a husband of mine dared to so much as flirt with another woman, I would . . . I would . . .'

'What?' Benjamin asked with good humour.

'Leave him immediately!' Faith answered emphatically.

'I shall bear that in mind.' Benjamin smiled at Faith, but both their faces showed instant shame when they looked back at Prudence.

'If you two children have finished sparring, I have no more time here to waste. If you are coming with us Faith, then you must do as I say and not speak a word out of turn. This is a personal visit between two women, not two adversaries. In fact, I hope we shall yet become friends of a sort.'

'Friends?' Faith repeated amazed at the thought. 'With 'that' sort?'

'Hopefully, yes.' Prudence walked her horse on until they were near to the lower road. There waiting for her was Madame Fleur sitting on a gig. Benjamin dismounted and Faith watched him as he confidently strode over to her. He secured the gig and pointed back to where Prudence was within the shadows of the trees.

'Mother, she looks pale, should we not ride out to her?' Faith asked quietly.

'No, Faith, it is not safe for us to risk being seen here. The fact that she has come all this way to us, in her obvious discomfort, tells me we are indeed going to be friends.' Prudence turned to face Faith, 'We have a mutual enemy.'

'Father?' Faith asked realising that he was the monster who must have treated Fleur so ill. 'Mother, what would he do to you if he found out about this rendezvous?'

Prudence shook her head, 'It is best not to think like that. We must do what we need to if your life is not to be ripped from you before it has properly begun. Now please, ride your horse over there, keep your eyes on the road, and make sure that you are not seen by anyone. You may listen to what we say, but on no account interrupt us at any point.'

Faith nodded and walked her horse to where she had a clear view of everything. Madame Fleur reached the shelter of the woods and leaned against an oak tree to catch her breath.

Prudence moved forward; her horse neighed as they approached and the emotionless eyes of Madame Fleur fixed on Prudence — in particular the crop she held within her right hand.

'You must excuse me, madam, for not dismounting, but I fear that without a mounting block I should not be able to remount as easily. I am not as agile as I once was.' Faith saw her mother's sincere expression; she was looking very concerned at the other lady's neck. 'Please understand I mean you no harm.'

'Why do you want to see me, Mrs

Wild. No games, please. What is it you want? Or is this whole charade no more than a ruse to shame me even more than your husband has already.'

Her voice was harsh, but it was unsure, unlike the calm confident manner she had had in her shop. Faith realised there was raw hurt in her words.

'I risked this meeting to offer you, firstly, my apology; I had not foreseen that my visit to your establishment should end in this.' She gestured to the bruising on Fleur's neck and cheek.

'I thought you had planned it, so that it would.' There was a note of resignation in Fleur's words that made Faith wonder if her spirit had in some way been broken. She opened her mouth to offer her support and condemnation of her father, but remembered her mother's clear order and decided not to.

'No, Letty, I hold nothing against you for you have saved me from the same fate. If I am honest with you, I owe you a lot.' Prudence looked quite emotional.

'You know my real name?' Fleur was visibly shocked.

'Yes, and much more — your past, from the wretched poorhouse, to den of iniquity, to my own husband, Oberon Wild.' Prudence was relaxed in her manner despite the gravity of her words. 'I am not here to judge you, Letty, because you have been given a sad start to your life and even now have not managed to cast it off, no matter how hard you have tried. I believe you nearly succeeded.'

'Get to the point then, ma'am. What is your second reason for this meeting?' Fleur was holding her sides firmly.

'Would you like to fill part of that order, now that you have no others to fill?' Prudence looked at her with compassion.

'How, precisely, am I to do that? With what? He will not pay for anything now.' She was standing straight again and Faith could see how much she would love to do that, given the chance.

'I will pay for it. I have the means, but first we must agree how it is to be done. If one falls we all fall, and you have already tasted the man's temper. When you return to town, send word to Mrs Bickerstaff that you are unwell and are leaving to visit relations in Skipton. That will keep the gossips happy, then pack up your needles and the minimum of clothes you would need to stay for a few weeks and await Benjamin's knock. He will take you to a place of safety, but you need to pack a large bag, not a trunk. Remember to pack the tools of your trade . . . '

'To which one do you refer?' Fleur answered sarcastically.

'The only one that will save us both, do you understand me? This is not a game for either of us.' Prudence's tone and manner was sharp. The other woman responded by nodding in agreement, suitably rebuked.

'Good, now do not speak of your past again. It is not an issue between us; it is our futures that count. Tomorrow we are to go to Harrogate. We shall collect you en-route. Be very careful, Letty. If any of us are to have a future we must agree to act and think as one.'

'You can trust me, woman. I've had enough of him and his type, but how do I know that I can trust you?' Letty stood next to the horse and stared imploringly at Prudence.

Prudence looked over to Faith. 'Yes, you know you can,' she answered simply and the other woman nodded in agreement. They shook hands and Madame Fleur returned swiftly to her gig.

Faith waited for Benjamin to come back safely.

'They take great risks for us,' Faith said quietly to him.

'I know, but I believe we are worth it. He winked at her and she smiled at him before rejoining her mother who was anxious that they return to the Hall immediately.

Oberon was restless. He sacked a worker for insolence for looking twice in his direction as he stormed through the mill and then threatened him with a beating for protesting at his harsh judgement.

Dermid stopped the mill worker from following Oberon back into the mill buildings and starting a fight.

Oberon slammed every door shut behind him, oblivious to the threat. 'Damn women! Damn them to hell and back!' he shouted as he swept everything that was on his immaculately laid out desk on to the floor in an unruly heap.

'Wilson! Wilson!' He yelled at the top of his voice for his clerk to come.

The nervous man crept silently around the office door. 'Yes, sir?' He saw the heap of paper and ink on the floor. All his carefully copied out letters ruined as they were covered in spilled ink. His face looked crestfallen.

'Tidy this bloody mess up and have those papers redrafted by tomorrow, first thing!' Oberon growled out his order.

'But . . . but . . . '

Oberon shoved a chubby finger towards the man's face. 'Never 'but' me, lad. Do it or I'll dock a day's pay from you for time-wasting.' Oberon barged past Wilson and out again. He did not hear the solitary word that passed Wilson's lips, questioning Wild's legitimacy.

Oberon stormed outside. He didn't know where to go or what to do next. He needed his Letty. He wanted her to hold him tightly, to whisper Obee in his ear, but she would not be ready to do that again for a few days. He thought of turning to his wife, but the thought of feeling her stiffen at his touch turned him towards the ale house.

Women were weak and hapless wretches. He'd drink the remains of his mood away then, when Fleur's bruises had gone, he'd buy her something and tell her she could reopen her shop.

That would put her right with him, so long as she never dare lay a finger on his beloved Faith again. But for now he would make do with the company of men and a fine bottle of brandy.

Prudence made all the necessary arrangements for them to travel to Harrogate the next day. She trusted Benjamin with the task of making sure that Letty was safely delivered to their coach at the agreed time in the morning. She had Cook make up some eats for the journey and Faith was given the task of locating some salve for the woman's bruises.

'Faith, dear, I want you to keep this hidden until we are in Harrogate.' Prudence held her hand out towards her.

Faith looked as her mother revealed a small pouch.

'Do not open it or lose it as it is a part of our future.' Faith nodded and placed it safely in her pocket. When the carriage arrived outside there was a huge commotion followed by her father being carried in by two of his men, inebriated and still swearing and cursing obscenities against women. It was with some surprise that Faith saw her mother smile at her.

As soon as he was taken to his room Prudence winked at her daughter. 'Oh, how brilliant this is! He will not wake till mid-day tomorrow for sure, and then he will be in a monster of a mood, but he shall have no recall of agreeing to us staying a night in Harrogate. Have Beth pack an overnight bag for us whilst I write a note to him thanking him for his generosity for allowing us to indulge ourselves.'

'Mother! Are you sure you know what you are doing? What will he say when he realises he has been duped?' Faith asked, as she felt the excitement rise within her.

'Nothing, because he won't realise, besides what can he say? He told us to be gone and stay away, enjoy ourselves . . . you heard him, didn't you? He wanted to be rid of the fairer sex for a while. We are merely following his orders. You do as I ask whilst I see he is settled and accept his generosity.'

8

Faith was woken early the next morning by her maid and she soon discovered her mother was already dressed and breakfasted. Benjamin, who had already loaded their case on to the back, brought the coach to the front of the hall.

Faith wasted no time. She ate as quickly as she could and joined her mother who waited in the morning room. When Faith entered, she thought that Prudence looked slightly unsure of herself, nervous even, at the action she was about to take. Anxiously, she paced back and forth in front of the large ornately-designed fireplace.

'Good, you are ready. We shall be on our way without hesitation. I've looked in on your father and he sleeps soundly. I doubt he has stirred all night long. Now, you must wear your warmest pelisse today and then we shall go.' Prudence smiled but Faith could sense her growing unease.

'Are you certain you wish to do this, Mother? It is not too late to call it off.' Faith stepped close to Prudence and whispered into her ear. 'There is no need to involve you in this. I could elope with Benjamin and we could send for you when we were settled down somewhere.'

Faith was shocked when her mother grabbed both of her arms firmly. 'Faith, promise me you would never do such a thing! You have no idea what danger you could place yourself in. No, we must stay together until you are settled and then if you wish me to be around you still, then I shall continue to be with you.'

'Of course I would want you to be around . . . what do you think, Mother? That I want rid of you? Never, that will not happen, ever!' Faith hugged her and she thought she heard a stifled sob from her mother's chest.

'No, I don't think for one moment you do, but you are so young still, don't close all the doors before the first one has truly opened. Now, we are wasting far too much time here.' Prudence picked up her reticule and sent Faith for her coat and hat.

Within moments Benjamin was helping them into the coach. 'Drive carefully, Ben. We are well within our estimated time.'

'Yes, ma'am,' he answered Prudence, and winked at Faith as he bent to help her climb inside.

She blushed slightly as much at the thought of what she had suggested to her mother only moments before. Did she really know him enough to run away with the man? The idea did not displease her, but she was aware that it could well be a foolishly brave act. Faith concentrated her mind back to their current subterfuge and decided it alone carried risk enough for her.

The coach made a steady pace as it

left Wildermill Hall behind and headed for the open road across the moor. The two women sat in silence. Each appeared to be lost within their thoughts. The movement halted and Prudence looked anxiously out of the coach window. 'What is it?'

'Beggin' yer pardon, Mrs Wild.' The figure of Dermid appeared as he rode his horse alongside their vehicle. 'I was lookin' for someone and was on my way to report their absence to Mr Wild, when I saw 'is coach comin' out so early in the mornin' like. I thought it may be Mister Wild 'imsel' out on business, surprisin' though, as he may be a little under the weather this morn.'

'Mr Wild is indeed 'under the weather' and is still in fact under his blankets. He will not be requiring your services until noon at least, I should take a guess. Perhaps you should call again then.'

The man looked quite pleased at the thought of having a morning off, although he had positioned himself close enough to see who was inside the coach.

'Now, tell me who this person is that you are seeking and we shall keep our eyes open for them along the road as we travel.'

The man did not answer straight away.

'Who is it you are looking for at this early hour, man?' Prudence asked, and Faith saw the corner of Dermid's lip curl up slightly.

'Oh, no-one of your acquaintance, ma'am.' His manner made Faith think it must be Letty the man was trying to find.

'Then please waste no more of our time. We have a journey to make and wish to travel whilst the weather is still fine. Good day, Mister.' Prudence answered the man abruptly.

He nodded politely and slowly pulled his horse away. The carriage moved on, but as the road bent around to follow the contour of the woods, Faith could see he was still watching their progress.

'What do we do if he follows us? What if he sees her, Mother? What . . . ' Faith was surprised when the coach picked up speed.

'What if you leave it to Benjamin. I'm sure he will know what to do,' Prudence said calmly.

'You sound as though you have known him for a long time. I don't understand how you could, Mother. We have always been kept separate from the townsfolk.' Faith looked at her. 'It's time I knew the secrets you are holding in your heart.'

'He is as dear to me as any son of my own could be. I've known his aunt since I moved here, Faith. Sarah shared with me a secret so shocking to me as a young bride, that I nearly fainted. Yet it saved me living in years of ignorance and pain. In some ways it prepared me for what was to come.'

'What could be so awful?' Faith asked, thinking what she knew of her father already was bad enough.

'Your father was young and success-ful. He built on what his father had started and his mill grew each year until he had closed down all the mills whose business was in opposition to his.

'He became conceited, an emotion I mistakenly took to be confidence when we first met and he wanted to impress me and my father to gain more capital for his planned expansion, as I was sheltered from his past. Your father had an older bother. The man was a villain, a gambler. He made your father look good by comparison.'

'Then he must have been vile,' Faith said and flinched slightly as Prudence shot her a look of disapproval that she should openly speak in such a way.

'He inherited his father's home and estate and a large sum of money, but he was a gambler, as I said, and could not hold on to money for long. Worse still, he was also a drunkard and a womaniser.

'On his last visit here he saw Benjamin's mother, a sweet, pretty girl.

She was flattered by the kind gentleman who offered her sweetmeats and trinkets, but he had only one thing in his mind.' Prudence sighed heavily.

'You don't mean that Benjamin is my cousin?' Faith asked, shocked at the thought that he should have been born as the result of such a man's sin.

'Yes.' Prudence nodded 'Unfortunately, I do.'

'But did Father know this? Does Benjamin know the truth?' Faith thought about how much her father had wanted a son of his own and what a vengeful person he was, so surely he would have claimed Benjamin in some way if he had.

'Your father has no idea of the truth, nor should he. Neither did his brother. The man died, in a drunken stupor I was informed, by your father. I do not know the details, and the secret of Benjamin's real father would have died with Ben's mother had it not been for Sarah being there in the last moments of her life. She begged Sarah to take him in and never to let the Wilds lay claim to him.'

'So does Benjamin know the truth?' Faith repeated. If he did, she wondered why he didn't hate them all.

'Yes, he does. Sarah and I told him when we were sure of his good character. After we explained to him why he was always that little bit different to the rest of his mother's family, he agreed that for his own sake he should keep the truth to himself. He also agreed not to make any wild claims to the family's fortune which has brought nothing but sadness to all who have touched it.

'So instead, we have devised a plan to give him and you the start in life you both deserve.' Prudence patted her daughter's knee affectionately.

'Please tell me the details of this plan or I shall not be able to concentrate on anything, Mother?' Faith pleaded with her. 'Surely I have the right to know, as you say, this is my life.'

'Yes, the time is here to explain,

before we pick up Letty Rose,' Prudence agreed.

'Letty Rose, is that her real name?' Faith asked whilst twisting her face as she repeated the name.

'It is the only one she was given by the poorhouse. You cannot blame her for believing Madame Fleur sounded very fine, it was infinitely better. Sarah and I have sufficient funds between us to purchase enough suitable attire for us to take you two far away to the new lands being developed in Australia. We are making arrangements to purchase the passages and a piece of land there.

'It will not be easy but she has a brother, a priest also, who has already established a church out in this wild land. He is prepared to help us all settle in once we arrive. It will be a month or so before everything is in place for us to travel so we must be very careful not to do anything out of the ordinary, other than prepare you for your coming wedding and appear to follow, a little reluctantly, your father's wishes.'

Prudence smiled at her and Faith could see a deep desire to fulfil this journey herself. Her mother's eyes betrayed a spark of hope at the prospect of their forthcoming freedom.

'It is so grand an idea that I dare not even contemplate travelling around the world. Is it really possible?' Faith asked, her stomach fluttering with excitement and her heart filled with joy at the thought. She had longed to travel and had always envied the freedom of men who could come and go at will — well, the gentry, anyway.

'Yes, I believe it is. Benjamin will travel with us, but you will behave as a lady, Faith. This is no elopement, this is your future. Keep your options open until you have seen for yourself the man he truly is. No-one must force your hand into a marriage except yourself; even then it should not be an act of force, but one of free will.'

'But you said yourself that you love him as you would your own son. Now you speak as if you are unsure,'

Faith protested slightly in defence of Benjamin.

'I do, Faith. But I am also old enough to know that a young man who has been chained into a life that ill suits him can change once those invisible bonds are replaced by the right to make choices of his own. Perhaps I am just untrusting of men. I think more of Benjamin than nearly any other man I have ever known.'

'Except your father, I presume.' Faith saw a strange, almost distant expression cross her mother's face.

'You presume wrongly.' Prudence gazed out of the window and Faith was filled with curiosity as to who this person was.

'Then who?' she asked.

'A friend, a very dear one.' Prudence snapped herself from her thoughts and stared at Faith as if focussing on the present and shaking off a memory from the past. 'Now let us speak no more of this. We shall be stopping soon and be on your guard. I will discuss what needs to be done regarding Madame Fleur. You listen quietly, for now.'

Faith hugged her mother until the coach slowed. Benjamin turned up a steep wooded track, and they ground to a steady halt. Ben's face soon appeared at the door.

'If you ladies would wait here a moment I shall make sure it is safe to pick up our passenger.' He smiled broadly at both of them, and Prudence opened her mouth to speak. 'Yes, ma'am, I shall take great care.'

Prudence shook her head. 'Impudent at times, but he always appears to be quite good humoured,' she admitted.

Faith watched as his agile figure disappeared into a forest path. Within minutes he returned carrying a leather bag, which he placed on the coach before returning. It was with some humour that Prudence and Faith saw him appear a second time carrying the delicate figure of Letty in his arms so she did not muddy her shoes or skirts.

'A born gentleman, even if he is the

illegitimate child of a Wild,' Prudence said.

'Mother,' Faith stared anxiously at Prudence before they neared the coach, 'You have no secrets to tell me regarding my own parentage, have you?' The thought had crossed her mind suddenly and filled her with a mixture of emotions, fear and, she had to admit . . . hope.

Prudence looked shocked. Her ill-timed question and the suggestion it raised had completely flustered Prudence. As Benjamin and Letty neared, all Prudence could do was stare blankly back at Faith, but her words failed her.

'Mother, am I or am I not Oberon's child?' Faith sat close to her mother but the coach door opened and his mistress joined them. Benjamin quickly settled back to his seat and was swift to take them on their way.

Madame Fleur sat on the opposite seat and once she had sorted out her skirts she looked from one to the other. Prudence was still a little pale and Faith wished she had picked her time better to question her mother.

If she wasn't his child then she would have to know who she was, and if he was, then she had insulted her mother in a very cruel way. Either way, she regretted speaking out. She elbowed her mother in the side, discreetly she hoped, and Prudence rallied.

'Are you feeling slightly better this morning, Madame?' Prudence asked, adopting her usual manner in which she spoke to Oberon. It covered up her feelings and thoughts to all who knew her well, and Faith had always taken great pride in thinking she was the only person who really did.

'Fine, I've been worse.' Letty laughed as Faith raised a shocked brow. 'Oh, girl, you have had a charmed life. Never mind, I wish mine had been so. Now, call me Letty between us, and tell me what it is you want and how you intend to keep that brute off my back.'

'By keeping you and your back well away from him. If you will content yourself by maintaining a very low profile whilst staying in a very nice cottage on the outskirts of the town, then you shall be safe and out of harm's way.'

Faith listened as Prudence detailed the outfits they would require, for which a price was agreed.

'Then what?' Letty asked. 'When my work is done, where do I go then?'

'Wherever you wish. You can travel to any town and you will have enough to set up a small business of your own. All you'll need to do is change your name again and work hard.' Prudence watched Letty laugh.

'Oh, I know how to work.'

'Then do it, woman, with pride that you will be working for yourself and no-one else this time,' Prudence said and issued the challenge.

Letty nodded in agreement. 'Thank you. You are not a bit like I imagined you to be.'

'I suppose my husband painted a picture of a pathetically weak woman with no brain of her own,' Prudence answered in a defiant tone that Faith had rarely heard.

'How well you know him,' Letty agreed.

'Yes, but there is much about me he never could be bothered to find out. That is Oberon Wild, a man with harsh foresight when it comes to his 'business' of bleeding people dry, but blind to what is happening under his own nose because he always underrates those around him, particularly women.

'When he wants something, he expects his ideas to bear fruit or he uses force, like a bully, to secure his way. But Oberon cannot control everything and everyone, nature does not bend to his will.' Prudence stopped and Letty sat back relaxed in their company. Faith felt uneasy, until her mother put her hand in hers.

'I should not complain, though, for I have been blessed with a beautiful daughter who has filled my life with joy. He calls her 'Oberon's Child', but this girl is almost a woman now and will be her own person, free of him, to find her own way and happiness in this life. No, Faith, open Cook's basket and we shall indeed enjoy this journey.'

9

It was with high spirits and a feeling of relief that all three arrived safely at a little cottage nestled in a croft of trees near the small winding river. As Benjamin opened the door and rolled down the step, Faith eagerly climbed down, holding his hand to balance. The two older women exchanged knowing looks as Faith had blushed slightly as soon as the two came into physical contact with each other.

The cottage door opened and an old lady with a lace cotton bonnet appeared at the doorway.

'Benjamin! My, my, you do look smart in that uniform. Come here and give your granny a big hug.' Her smile lacked a few teeth, but it was filled with warmth and love. Benjamin duly obliged then glanced apologetically back to the ladies who watched on.

Faith took this show of open affection as further proof, if it were needed, that Benjamin was a good man. She looked on in anticipation of the day when those strong arms would lift her off the ground as he did the old lady. Prudence, Faith could tell, also approved, but there was a more sombre look on the face of Letty.

How many arms had held her, Faith wondered, yet shown her no tender emotion, innocent but life giving love? The woman looked at her and grinned nervously, as if she did not quite know what to do.

Benjamin returned to her with his grandmother on his arm.

'So you are the young lady who has stolen away my Benjamin's heart, eh?' She looked sternly at Faith, who held her glare.

'I hope I did not steal it, ma'am, as I'd prefer it was given willingly.' Faith saw the old lady's face break out into laughter.

'Ay lad, she's fair enough. Now then,

this lady must be her good mother,' she turned to Prudence, 'and this . . . ' she looked Letty up and down. The woman put her shoulders back and was obviously waiting for an insult of some kind.

'And this must be the lady seamstress you told me about.' She walked over to Letty. 'My dear young woman. You shall share my cottage with my blessing and my home baking whilst you work on the trousseau. You shall be safe here from further accidents.'

Before anyone else could speak she insisted they all had some homemade pie and a cup of her best tea. Especially Benjamin who had a double portion.

Although small, the cottage was extremely neat and had samplers adorning the walls. Her bed and chairs were covered in home quilted throws and her oak table was laid with embroidered linen cloths.

The wooden floor was covered with clip rugs and a fireplace, cauldron and bread oven took centre place along the end wall.

It was both homely and cosy. The stairs to the side of the entrance, Faith realised, must lead to her sleeping area.

'My home is humble, miss . . . '

'Letty, ma'am, please call me Letty. It is a lovely home, like I've always imagined a proper home should be.' Faith watched her as she admired the stitching on an embroidered cushion. 'You are a very skilled lady.'

Faith saw a flush of colour appear in the woman's face and she realised how much this worldly woman really meant her words.

'Well, you are welcome to share it whilst you work. I chatter on a bit, but then I don't get many visitors and I don't get into town as oft as I used to.' The old lady looked at Benjamin. 'Perhaps I may even be able to be of some help to someone at last.'

'You would be most welcome to do so, Mrs Bellowby,' Letty said with some enthusiasm.

'I'm sorry that we cannot stay longer, Mrs Bellowby, but we really have to carry on with our journey to Harrogate. We shall call on our return tomorrow and drop off further supplies for you both.' Prudence stood up.

'Further supplies?' Letty asked.

'Yes, Benjamin removed some of the stock from your shop last night. I hope you understand why we had to act so secretly. I shall let you know tomorrow when we are required to come back for the fittings. Then we shall of course come here first on our return journey.'

Benjamin brought Letty's bag in and placed it upstairs, then produced some fabric from Madam Fleur's own stock.

'You have done well, Mrs Wild. You seem to have thought of everything,' Letty said with admiration.

'I hope so, but we must not stay here any longer. Until tomorrow . . . ' She shook Mrs Bellowby's hand and walked outside the cottage.

Faith gave the lady a hug. 'Thank you so much for agreeing to do this for us.'

'This is no trouble. I was feeling bored, anyhow. You just look after my Benjamin for me. Treat him right, lass.'

'I will.'

Faith left as Benjamin placed a protective hand on her shoulder and walked her to the door.

He stepped back and gave his grandmother a big hug, and she giggled in his arms. 'Be off with you!'

He left to help Prudence and Faith into the carriage.

'How I envy them,' said Letty.

'Wait till you get to my age, lass, you'll envy everything that can move at its own will.'

As Faith glanced back she saw Mrs Bellowby and Letty exchange glances and laugh.

'It looks as though they will get on with each other, Mother,' she said reassuringly.

'I should think they will, you don't raise eight children and bury four without learning a lot about surviving. They are both life scholars. I should think they will have much of interest to talk about.'

Faith sat down in the carriage and pondered how hard just living was for so many people around her, yet realising how simple and straightforward hers had always been until lately.

'So, Mother you were about to tell me about my father . . . ' Faith began, but her mother's face darkened.

'Faith, I am doing as much for you as I can. You are Oberon's child! Be content and do not question me on this matter again.' She closed her eyes and rested her head back on the upholstered seat. The subject and the conversation ceased.

★   ★   ★

From the moment they arrived at the grand hotel, Prudence swept into action as a confident matriarch. She had their bag taken up to a sumptuous room, ordered dinner for later in the day, whilst she sent Benjamin off to stable the horse and carriage.

Faith was so excited, everything was so elegant. They were served a light repast and then readied themselves for yet more measuring and ordering from the outfitter of her husband's choice.

She had been given a reduced list, edited by Oberon himself, about a third of the original. However, that was of no importance now as Letty had the measurements she needed to prepare their order for the journey they had planned.

Benjamin summoned a gig for them to make the journey. Prudence handed him a purse and leaned over to him. 'Buy yourself some decent clothes so that you may join us for dinner and see to what you need for the journey.' He nodded and left without looking at Faith. She felt slightly downcast as he seemed far from pleased to take the purse from Prudence.

Prudence shook her head at him as he walked away. 'Pride is a stubborn master.'

Four hours later they finally returned to the hotel. 'Mother, we should be ready for dinner. We must rush!'

'Oh, Faith! I have no more rush in me. You shall put on your dress and eat dinner in the restaurant; I shall have a light meal brought to my room. I am quite exhausted.' Prudence linked arms with Faith who was most concerned.

'How can I eat alone, Mother?' Faith asked in disbelief.

'You won't be. I've invited Benjamin to join us. You will have to make do with eating with him.' Prudence did not look at Faith, but she sensed the woman was still plotting and planning. Far from being exhausted or weak she was being discreet and match-making into the bargain.

Within the hour Faith was dressed from head to toe in her finest dress, shoes, jewels, and her hair had been set high by a hotel maid. She felt like a princess and walked with elegance and confidence.

Prudence walked with her to the top

of the stairs that overlooked the grand hotel entrance. They looked around amongst the well attired people who walked from the lounge to the restaurant.

Faith tapped her mother's arm as a handsome man entered the hotel, his tall frame showing off the line of the new jacket and trousers to perfection. His mass of blond hair had been cut into a shorter and more fashionable style. At first he looked around him, and then, as if he sensed he was being watched, he turned to face them.

'I think I shall retire now, Faith,' Prudence said, but Faith just stared back at Benjamin who was making his way up the stairs towards them.

'Faith!' Prudence snapped her attention back to her.

'Yes, Mother, did you say something?' Faith asked, still watching Ben.

'I'm going now,' Prudence said but tapped Faith's arm. 'For goodness sake, girl, please shut your mouth and remember where you are.'

Faith blushed and looked at her mother. 'Sorry, Mother, it was just that I . . . ' Faith felt embarrassed.

'I know what it is, Faith, but please remember where you are. Do not disgrace yourself.' She left as Benjamin took Faith's hand and led her towards the dining-room.

'A discreet table for two,' he asked the head waiter and passed him a coin. They soon found themselves seated in a little alcove on the outside of the restaurant surrounded on three sides by luscious foliage.

Faith was seated first and, after they ordered, their precious moment of privacy arrived.

'You look beautiful, Miss . . . ' Benjamin stumbled over his words. He obviously hated this subservient position; he wanted to call her Faith.

'Faith, Benjamin, or I shall have to call you, what? Mr . . . ' she saw that he understood her meaning.

'I am what I am, Faith. I can not change that. Does it affect your opinion of me? I would prefer it did not in either way, good or bad.' His eyes showed the depth he truly meant his words.

'Benjamin, why don't you hate me and my family for what they did to your mother? Your father did,' Faith asked quietly.

'Because, Faith, strange as it seems, I have benefited from this hateful act. I would have a drunkard for a true father, and been brought up in the mill and on the streets. Instead I have known what it is to have a loving decent family, an education and to watch a beautiful girl grow into a woman who I both respect and love.'

He squeezed her hand, but as a waiter appeared it was quickly withdrawn as their first course was served. They sat silently until their privacy was secure once more.

'Do you think Mother's plan will work, Ben? If not, I dread to think what Father will do to us all.' Faith watched his eyes light up with the impish mischievous air that she had seen so many times at church.

'It will succeed, Faith, because it has to. We will all have this amazing adventure to engage in beyond the reach of Oberon Wild. By the time he is aware that we have all deserted him, we will be half way around this magnificent world.' His eyes were bright, obviously excited at the prospect.

Faith smiled. 'I am frightened at the thought, yet cannot wait for the day we set sail.'

'Eat up, Faith. We shall have some time to ourselves before I return you safe and sound to your mother once more.' Benjamin winked at her and Faith laughed at his manner. He was so different to her father, and then her smile dropped.

'What is it?' Benjamin instinctively knew something troubled her.

'I am Oberon's child. I wish I wasn't.' She looked down sadly.

'I don't care whose child you were, Faith. You are a woman now and soon will be my wife. No-one will stand in our way. Past is past, we are the future.'

Faith stared at him. He had such a clear foresight that she felt a thrill when he spoke to her in such a way, yet there was a part of her that cried out not to be a daughter or a wife, just to be her own Faith.

10

Oberon awoke with a head that felt as though a horse had kicked it. The room was bright, far too bright for him to open his aching swollen eyes. He realised it was flooded with daylight.

For a while he laid there motionless, letting his senses gradually come back to him. What had he been doing the previous evening? He realised what, but it took him a while to recall where. Slowly he remembered the club, the men he'd been drinking with.

Baxter, the blacksmith, had been with him. He had drunk Oberon under the table as usual. He never could out-drink the man, not with brandy, anyway. Where had Dermid been? Oh yes, he had helped him into the carriage that had brought him home. That was the last memory he had of the evening. Beyond that all was blackness itself.

After some time he opened his eyes and focused on the room. The curtains were drawn making the colours seem more vibrant as his eyes adjusted. A tray had been left on his bedside table with a jug of water and a powder for his stomach. He sat up, swayed and nearly fell back down. It was daylight.

The thought appalled him as he should have been in his office to see if that idle clerk of his had rewritten the papers he had asked for. Yes, he remembered that, and vaguely he remembered the longing to see his Rose again — 'Madame Fleur' as she now called herself. He spluttered a mocking gesture at the thought of Letty Rose being a 'lady' to respect. He should never have set her up in a shop of her own.

No, he decided, it would be far better if she concentrated her time on him and lived in their rooms. She had become far too proud and everyone knows what that comes before.

Oberon drank the water infused with

the powder then slowly stood up. He ignored the ache in his head, knowing it would lift eventually. A note, in Prudence's handwriting, had been propped on his bedside table. He opened it and focussed his eyes on her perfectly-written script.

My Dear Sir,
Thank you so much for your unselfish generosity. Faith and I will enjoy ordering her revised trousseau from such a well thought of establishment. Faith was delighted at your suggestion that we stay the night in a hotel and return refreshed tomorrow. You have made us both very happy indeed. Until tomorrow evening, my best wishes.
Yours, Prudence.

His hand shook as he re-read the note. When had he had any notion of giving them permission to stay a whole night away from home? Had he lost leave of his senses?

Perhaps he had been so repulsed by the sight of Prudence's pious demeanour that he had sent her away. Whatever the reason for this offer, he took some solace from the thought that he had made Faith happy.

Prudence may as well enjoy this night with her daughter because in three weeks she would be married and travelling to the far-side of the world. He was glad he had not told them that the marriage date had been brought forward because of a development in his friend's speculating in Australia.

He would tell them as soon as they arrived back. That way he would catch Faith whilst she was still excited about her trousseau. He would send a message to the milliner to tell them to have the outfits ready to collect by a date three weeks hence if they wanted to receive their payment in full. There would be no need for fittings and things because they already had her measurements.

Immediately, he rang for his man-servant. Within the hour he had been washed, changed and breakfasted. He prided himself on his strong constitution. Dermid was summoned and Oberon's horse saddled. He had never been so late for the office before.

In fact, he had broken his routine more times recently than he cared to acknowledge. His world was falling apart, and that he would never stand by and watch happen.

Oberon and Dermid left Wildermill Hall together. Master ahead of servant. 'Once I am at the mill bring Letty straight to me. I have something I wish to tell her,' he ordered Dermid without taking the trouble to look at his servant. He did not see the uneven grin spread across the man's stubbled face.

'I'm afraid I cannot do that, sir.' Dermid said in a gentle Irish lilt.

'Why ever not? Explain yourself man!' Oberon stopped his horse and stared at the man as if he had lost leave of his senses.

'She has left town. Word 'as it that she has gone to recover from an illness

141

at a relative's over Skipton way,' Dermid replied keeping his face very sombre.

'Relative! What relative? She's an orphan. Her type don't have relatives. Find her, man, and drag her back here. Don't return without her!' Oberon's head throbbed as his voice and temper rose.

Dermid turned his horse around to head off up the road.

'What do you think you're doing?' Oberon shouted to him.

'I'm going to look for Fleur as you ordered . . . Sir.' Dermid answered, his arms crossed casually over his rifle in his usual relaxed manner.

'Not before I am established at the mill, you Irish . . . ' Oberon shook his head. 'Then find her and be sure to be here by six to collect me.'

Oberon walked his horse onwards.

'What if I can't locate her in that time . . . sir?' Dermid asked, a stern look on his face.

'Don't provoke me, man. You look again and again until you do, but find her you will!' Oberon kicked his horse into a canter nearly knocking a man over in the street.

Dermid followed silently behind.

Oberon dismounted and stormed off into the mill. Dermid caught the reins of the discarded horse and handed them to the stable lad who had run over to them. He looked up at the Irish man, who seemed in very poor spirits.

'Mr Dermid.' The lad stared at the brute of a man who raised a quizzical eyebrow at him.

'Yes, lad, what is it?' Dermid growled fuming at Oberon's off hand dismissal of him.

'Do yer think he would give Bill 'is job back? The man's in a right state.' The lad's sad eyes had no effect on Dermid, no more than they would have had on Oberon himself.

'Ay, lad, there's every chance ... ' Dermid laughed, 'when hell freezes over, that is, but not before.' Dermid laughed cynically and rode out of the gates.

'I'm sorry, Bill, I tried, but you know what 'e's like.' The boy turned to the shadows of the stable block where his friend had waited since dawn for Oberon to arrive at the mill. He had been prepared to beg if necessary to save his family further hardship, but Dermid's response made him see the futility of his situation.

The man, Bill, did not speak but sloped off into the shadows with an old pot of grease that he had been hiding in case his last resort failed . . . it had.

11

Faith had hardly slept. After the lovely meal the previous evening Benjamin had taken her for a walk along the hotel's carpeted corridors, talking and joking as they ambled along.

They had opened a door to what they had thought would lead them to the outside, hoping to extend the precious time by a saunter around the building within it's grounds, but in fact it was the door to a large, shelved linen cupboard.

Benjamin should have closed it as quickly as he could and returned to the busy main lounge. Instead, shamelessly, they had seized an opportune moment. One innocent kiss . . . a gentle caress became an embrace, and the passion of both Faith and Benjamin was openly shared for those few stolen moments.

The experience surprised and delighted

Faith. She had never felt so alive or driven. Propriety aside, she listened only to her heart and body. She had always known she loved him, from afar, but here up close it was an affirmation that he was definitely the man she wanted as a husband.

It was Benjamin who pulled away first. Faith felt disappointed that he had. Physically her body wanted to respond to his touch, but she had acted so brazenly that she must have shocked him? His colour was high; his usually calm manner was ruffled, flustered even.

He insisted that he should escort her back to Prudence before they were discovered and her reputation totally destroyed. So a perfect evening had ended in a surge of mixed emotions.

This morning, Prudence and Faith had breakfasted in an uneasy silence. Prudence seemed to have a cloud over her previous high spirits as she faced returning to Wildermill Hall. Faith was lost in her own memories of the previous evening and the caresses with which it had ended.

Benjamin was waiting outside. He greeted Prudence with a warm smile. She returned it in kind as she passed him by. Faith stared at him; he was back in his uniform, the coach ready and she remembered how fine he had looked dressed as a young gentleman.

When Prudence could not see his face, he winked at Faith and grinned broadly, and she knew he was her Benjamin, nothing had changed.

If anything it was a more intimate and familiar gesture than it had been previously. She wanted to hug him there and then, but remembered their situation and followed her mother.

There would be time enough for that in the coming months, once they returned to the milliners for her fittings and then when they departed for their new life. She would wait — what was two months when it was your whole life that you were planning for?

Dermid had three stiff drinks. He

147

knew Fleur had done a runner and admired her for taking the chance to get away from Wild. She was too good for Oberon. He had already searched high and low for her with no success. He was delighted at the thought of how she would have had to persuade him not to divulge her whereabouts to Wild, the half grin appeared on his face, but she had disappeared without a trail or trace.

So with no hope of producing her as an offering to appease his 'master' and with the growing abuse of his Irish blood, Dermid had decided to take matters into his own hands. But he needed an alibi. He went over to the bar, deliberately knocking a man's drink over as he did.

'Oi! Take care,' the man protested.

Dermid rounded on him, grabbing the man's throat in one hand and slowly squeezing it.

'Dermid! Dermid! Calm down, man!' The innkeeper ran around the bar's counter and pushed between the two men. 'It was an accident; no need for any fights now, is there?' A bead of sweat was appearing on the innkeeper's brow. 'Joseph, pour these men new drinks and, gentlemen, please enjoy them on the house.'

Dermid released the man, who accepted the free drink happily and moved far away from Dermid.

'Thanks,' Dermid said to the inn-keeper as he swallowed his down. 'Give me a jug of ale. I'll be over in the corner, left in peace I hope.'

'Very well, Dermid. I shall see you are not disturbed.' The innkeeper watched Dermid walk over to the dark corner at the back of the inn. It was where people went for a discreet word or a bit of privacy.

The jug was brought over with a tankard and Dermid grunted his thanks. He was left alone. Within minutes he had slipped out of the back of the inn and skirted around the shadows of the narrow streets slipping easily back inside the mill grounds. The noise of the machines clattering inside echoed on the air.

He made his way to Oberon's private stairs that led up to his office and drew his lethal skinning knife from under his greatcoat. Oberon had thrown his last insult at him.

Soon, with money from the man's pockets, he would be headed home to his beloved Ireland. It was with these driven thoughts that he nimbly ran up the iron stairs. In the dark seclusion of this covered stairwell he knew his way, but he failed to see the spilled tin of grease on the top three steps.

If he had been stepping slowly he would have been saved, but he had to do his task quickly and return before his absence was noted and his alibi blown. He ran at them, slipped, tumbled and fell, landing on the ground atop his own knife. Dermid would not be returning anywhere.

Oberon thought he heard a noise on the stairs. So the woman had returned. He'd make sure she never ran again.

Dermid must have found her. He opened the door, but could not see down to the bottom clearly or hear anyone in the dim light.

He leaned forward. 'Is anyone there? Speak now if you are or I'll set the dogs on to you.'

There was no answer. He locked the door. Must have been a cat or some animal, he thought.

Disappointed, he resumed his work. When it was time to leave he was even more troubled when Dermid did not return, even on his own.

'Damn the man!' he shouted at the young stable lad who gave him his horse. 'When he dares to arrive, lad, tell him Mr Wild says he is fired!' Oberon galloped out of the mill grounds along the narrow streets of the old town, but this time he did not have his man riding behind him, watching his back.

The first he was aware that he was being followed was when a hefty stone hit the back of his shoulder.

'What the . . . ' Oberon looked around furiously but could not see the hand that had thrown it.

'Ungrateful rabble,' he yelled. Another one flew in the air just missing his head. He kicked his horse to a canter.

The third stone hit his horse's rump sending it into a wild gallop. Oberon held on for dear life, cursing the perpetrator of this attack and the man, Dermid.

He rode the horse's panic out along the road. By the time he was at the gates of Wildermill Hall both horse and rider were in a sweat of exhaustion. Servants were summoned and the doctor, as his shoulder was badly bruised.

Oberon took to his bed. In truth, he was frightened. Without his man behind him he had come under open attack. He'd make them pay for this, whoever it was.

★　★　★

It was with haste that the carriage detoured to take the material that Letty needed back to the cottage.

When they arrived, the room had been turned into a workshop. Mrs Bellowby and Letty were both being as industrious as each other.

'Oh, this is beautiful,' Mrs Bellowby exclaimed as she inspected the new fabrics.

'You have done well,' Prudence replied enthusiastically. 'We shall be returning in one month. If we need to communicate further then I shall send Benjamin.'

'Oh, please do, I shall miss him, you know.' Mrs Bellowby hugged her grandson and he looked compassionately down at the older lady. Faith could tell the feeling was mutual and she felt a tinge of guilt that she was taking him away from the only family he had known and loved.

As they continued back to Wildermill she looked at her mother. 'This isn't fair. It's all Father's fault. He should be the one to leave. I wish he would, then we could clean up the mill, and the town and treat the people fairly.'

'My dear Faith, don't live in regrets for what can never be. Be grateful that at least you will be having the option of leaving and starting a new life away from him. Faith, life isn't fair, it is really quite hard but one has to make the most of what you are given in it.'

It was with that thought that Faith sat silently pondering all of their futures when she heard a rider approaching their coach at speed.

The coach stopped.

'What is it?' Prudence shouted to Benjamin. The rider dismounted and, holding his horse's reins in one hand, opened the door with the other to speak to Prudence directly.

'Whatever is the matter, Josiah?' Prudence asked. Faith was surprised that her mother seemed so at ease with the owner of the blacksmith's and the Ironmonger's.

'Oh, P . . . Mrs Wild. I was so

concerned for you. There has been a spot of trouble. The militia are all over the town. Dermid was found with a knife in him at the mill.

'It looks as though he caught someone on Mr Wild's private stairs, they fought and he was killed — Dermid that is. The murderer must have fled and when Mr Wild left the mill he came under further attack as stones were thrown by, we presume, the same man.'

Josiah was short of breath. Two of his men rode up carrying rifles.

'My men will escort you ladies safely back to the hall where Mr Wild is recovering from his ordeal.' He smiled warmly at Faith, 'Pardon this outburst, miss, but I'm all of a dither.'

'Is he well?' Prudence asked.

'Shaken, and he has a badly bruised shoulder, but nothing life threatening.'

Faith quickly looked down to hide the shame she had instantly felt at the thoughts that filled her head.

'Josiah, ride with us. You are shaking,'

Prudence offered and Faith looked at her mother's face that was all concern and compassion for this man. Her reaction was in stark contrast to the total lack of emotion which she had shown regarding her father's condition.

'Thank you, I will, just to the gates of the Hall.'

Benjamin took his horse, passing the reins to one of Josiah's men as he settled inside.

'My, what a beautiful daughter you have, Mrs Wild,' he said amiably and Faith saw the pride in her mother's eyes.

'You are too kind, sir,' Faith said rather awkwardly then watched out of the window whilst Prudence and Josiah engaged in polite conversation.

The rest of the journey passed uneventfully and it was with a sad countenance that they all returned to the hall which now had two soldiers from the militia adorning the door.

Prudence made her way up to Oberon's room. She knocked lightly, hoping he may be asleep.

'Come in!' the voice boomed. Prudence realised that he was not weak by the tone of the voice. Faith stayed on the landing outside. She could hear what was being said but did not wish to enter.

'So, madam, you have decided to return to your husband!' he bellowed accusingly.

'Oberon, dear, we were seeing the trousseau as you ordered we should . . . ' Prudence's voice was timid and quiet as usual, Faith had thought. A totally different voice to the one she had used for the last two wonderful days.

'And did I order you to go gallivanting overnight? Hmm? Answer me that!' he shouted.

'But you suggested it. We thought it was so kind and . . . '

'Yes, too kind, whilst I am nearly murdered. Not once but twice! By heavens, I hope they catch this maniac before the wedding party arrives. I . . . '

'Twelve weeks is a long time, my dear. I'm sure that they will do everything they can do . . .'

'No, madam, not twelve weeks! Not twelve weeks, but three. The date was brought forward to fit in with the export of the sheep.' Oberon's voice was calmer.

Faith grabbed hold of the door handle as much to support herself from the effect of this devastating news as to enter the room.

'Three weeks, Father! My trousseau will never be ready in time.' She looked at her mother who had gone quite pale again.

'It will be collected in time. I shall demand they speed up the order. Don't worry yourself on that account.' He dismissed her concerns.

'What about the fittings we need to return?' Faith was staring at her mother, desperate for her to say something.

'You, girl, are going nowhere until your husband takes you to his ship. You will stay within the hall for your own safety. A madman is on the loose and we have to prepare for the wedding. Neither of you will have need to leave Wildermill again until Faith goes in three weeks time.'

Wild sat up to stress his point and grimaced as pain shot through his shoulder and he flopped back on to his pillows.

He pointed to a jar of salve and said to Prudence, 'I need that rubbing on my back.'

Prudence put a comforting hand on Faith's shoulder and walked her stunned daughter to the doorway. 'I'll send up a maid,' she answered Oberon and closed the door quickly behind her before he could demand she administer his medication herself.

'Mother, what do we do now? Surely we are lost!' Faith looked anxiously at her mother.

'No, my child. We are temporarily thrown. But when one is lost then you either find your own way out or seek help,' Prudence said quietly and patted the girl's shoulder as they walked down the stairs to the morning room.

'So what do we do?' Faith asked, her spirit dashed by the thought of being wedded off and shipped to Australia with a herd of sheep.

'We ask for help. Something I perhaps should have done a long time ago, but did not dare to until now.' Prudence sat Faith down. 'I'll send a maid to your father and order a tray for us. I need time to think.'

She left Faith staring into the flames of a newly lit fire, despairing at the thought that time was the one thing they did not seem to have.

12

Prudence entered Oberon's study. She sat behind his large mahogany desk and removed the key from where it was hidden under the seat of his chair. He was a creature of habit, thankfully. Opening the narrow drawer in front of her she removed the last letter he had received from his daughter's intended.

Silently she took out some clean paper and positioned herself in order to write in her neatest script. The letter was unanswered. She knew this because he always tore off the top left hand corner of correspondence he had dealt with and then had it filed away. She would write her husband's reply.

Oberon never actually wrote his own letters. He found it tedious, he would say, often complaining that ideas were from bright minds, whilst committing them to paper was for the menial minded. The truth being he was a messy writer whose spelling was very poor. He paid others more able than he to write the words for him, so he could just sign the bottom.

Prudence took time to pray before she committed this desperate act, but she needed to buy herself and Faith time. She started to write.

It is with great sadness that I must . . .

No, that was not right. She threw the paper into the fire and sat herself down ready to try again, forcing herself to think like her husband.

I am writing to inform you that due to an unfortunate event at the Mill, I have been injured, and will not be able to accommodate the wedding party within three week's time. I find it extremely inconvenient and annoying that events have taken this sad turn.

I therefore can see no other alternative than for you to go on ahead with your plans to travel to Australia as our business insists you do. I shall personally escort my daughter to you within the year. This is definitely the best course of action to take or else you shall jeopardise our investment in the new land.

Yours sincerely,
Oberon Wild.

She carefully dated and sealed it before summoning Benjamin.

'Mrs Wild, if what I have heard is correct then our plans lie in ruins.' Benjamin was hardly in the room before he expressed his concern.

'No, they do not, but we must take even greater risks. I want you to send this letter with all haste. Then summon the doctor to me, and tell the Reverend that he must carry on with the planned wedding in three weeks' time. First, though come with me.'

She walked over to the morning

163

room and closed the door firmly behind them.

'Faith, Benjamin has a proposal to make to you and I wish to know the truth of your reply because everything hinges on your response.' Prudence looked at Benjamin and raised her eyebrows.

Benjamin took hold of Faith's hand in his. In a softly spoken voice he asked simply, 'Faith, will you be my wife? I love you with all my heart, but I cannot promise you a certain future . . . '

Faith placed a finger on his lips. 'Nothing in life is certain Benjamin, but if there is anyway out of this mess then I shall happily be your wife.' She looked at her mother. 'But how?'

'Benjamin send that letter on its way, tell Sarah and the good Reverend that it is you who will be married to Faith in three weeks, arrange the banns accordingly, then go to your grandmother's and advise her that the clothes will be needed earlier than expected.

'I shall write another letter to the

milliner's whilst you are gone, but be sure to have the doctor call. Tell them that Mr Wild is suffering the after-effects of the attack and will need something to calm his nerves and pain.'

Benjamin opened his eyes wide. 'You are not thinking of drugging him for three weeks surely?'

'At the moment I am considering all options. Take care Benjamin, there is a murderer out there and the militia are looking for someone to blame.'

'I will,' Benjamin hugged Faith and kissed her brow, 'we will wed, Faith.' He left swiftly.

Faith watched him ride down the drive. 'Mother, how on earth do you expect to fool Father for three weeks?'

'Once the wedding is announced on Sunday, I am hoping he will not reverse the decision 'if' he finds out.' Prudence looked down. 'Send the doctor up as soon as he arrives.'

To Faith's surprise it was the Reverend who arrived first. Faith showed him up to her father's room.

Prudence was seated in a chair in the corner of the room, whilst Oberon slept.

'Reverend!' Prudence stood up quickly, her voice a little louder than she should have spoken and it roused Oberon.

'My dear, Mrs Wild, I am delighted by this amazing news . . . Benjamin is . . . '

'Please, Reverend, keep your voice low.' She gestured towards Oberon who was rubbing his eyes.

'Reverend! Have they sent for you? Am I . . . ' Wild's face was white with fear. It was all Prudence could do not to laugh at his cowardice. One stone bruised his back and he was hiding in his bed like the world was after him.

'Please do not worry yourself, Mr Wild, I merely came straight here to say how delighted we all are at the prospect of the forthcoming union between these two lovely people.' He looked at Faith and smiled.

Faith was waiting for him to mention

Benjamin and throw them all into turmoil.

'As you can see I am hardly in a position to discuss it now. However, my wife will handle the arrangements, with my daughter's and your help.' Prudence and Faith stared at each other in disbelief. Could he really play into their hands unwittingly?

'Oh, do not worry yourself about the details. We shall do everything. You concentrate on your speedy recovery. Do you wish to delay the wedding a week or so to give you more time to mend, sir?' the Reverend offered, and Faith breathed in deeply, noticing the panic on her mother's face.

'Three weeks, man! I insist. They shall be wed in three weeks and no delay will be tolerated.' Oberon's old manner broke through. The Reverend stepped back and looked at Prudence.

'Yes, three weeks it shall be, I shall leave you to rest now, sir. Should you feel you need me, please send me a note and I shall come.' Prudence nodded at him as if he had made the correct decision to leave the man to his rest.

He left and Faith's heart lifted as, unwittingly, Oberon had just agreed to her wedding to Benjamin.

Shortly afterwards the doctor arrived. Oberon played the suffering wounded party well. Faith and Prudence had both realised that, as well as being a complete baby when coping with his own pain, he was scared to ride through the town without Dermid with him, even though the militia had offered to send a man to accompany him when he wanted to return.

When the doctor greeted Prudence and explained, 'I have left him a tonic and a draft to calm his nerves. He must take only the stated dose and he may feel drowsy, but he will be able to rest and recover. I expect he will be on his feet and back to his robust self within the week.'

'Good,' said Prudence with little conviction, although the doctor did not realise the sentiment was missing.

For one week Oberon sipped his tonic and draft and stayed within his room, it was only when the Captain of the militia announced that they had concluded their investigations and determined that the culprits had fled, that Oberon dressed and came rather shakily downstairs for breakfast.

It was Sunday and nothing would stop him from attending church to hear the banns of marriage read out for the second time. He wanted to know when the marriage party was arriving and what was happening at the mill in his absence.

Faith and Prudence were already eating their when Oberon entered the breakfast room. Both looked shocked and came to help him to his chair.

Faith was amazed how his clothes hung on him. He had lost weight and looked almost sallow in his complexion.

'Don't fuss, woman!' he snapped at Prudence.

She sat back down and looked at her food, as did Faith but both women

169

appeared to have lost their appetite.

'After church I shall be returning to the mill. I . . . ' Oberon began.

'You are not well enough to attend church, Father, surely not. You have been ill in bed a whole week. Perhaps you should leave it until next week, save yourself,' Faith began nervously.

'Absolutely not, I shall be there today.'

'I think not, dear. The coach is already here. It is time we left.' Prudence and Faith stood.

'But it can't be. The clock in my room . . . ' he looked at the longcase clock and realised . . . 'is nearly an hour slow!'

'Oh, what a shame and you had dressed, Father,' Faith said and headed for the door with her mother.

'Never mind. As you say I am dressed. I shall eat bread on the way and have a meal after the service. Come, or we shall be late.' Oberon led the way out into the hall. He was helped on with his coat that seemed to dwarf him now. Prudence and Faith were both looking very worried.

'Don't fuss, women. I am fine.' He led the way out and into the coach.

Faith realised he thought they were purely concerned with his health. However, disturbing and fragile as it appeared, he had no idea why they both looked so worried, but he was about to find out.

★   ★   ★

Inside the coach Faith was lost in thought. It was Oberon who took her mother's attention. He really did look pale and was hugging himself as if he was cold.

'Oberon, do you feel well?' Prudence asked.

'Of course I do woman, and stop fussing!' His abrupt reply rebuffed all other actions to make him more comfortable.

Josiah greeted them and offered Oberon his cane to steady himself, which surprisingly, he accepted. They entered the family pew with trepidation. Benjamin looked up and saw Oberon.

Faith and he stared blankly at each other. To the congregation it would appear to be concern for his well-being, but they both knew differently.

A voice echoed out across the Reverend as he opened the service.

'He has no right to be 'ere!' Bill ran forward. 'This is a place for good Christian men, and ... ' Before he could speak further, Josiah had him bodily removed. Prudence nodded her thanks, but Oberon had been shocked by the sudden surge forward of the man and had grabbed his chest.

His breath seemed short but, as all eyes turned from Bill to him, he motioned for the Reverend to continue.

The service progressed and Faith and Prudence gripped each other's hands tightly as the marriage of Faith Mary Wild to Benjamin Richard Lewis was announced.

Prudence and Faith waited for the eruption from Oberon, but it never happened. The service continued as no-one had given a reason why the wedding should not take place.

Faith and Prudence looked to each other and then to Oberon, who sat stock still, his eyes fixed ahead of him. A deathly pallor covered his face. Neither mother or daughter spoke. The congregation stood. Prudence gently tapped Oberon's shoulder and he crumpled to the floor, motionless. Faith screamed, Prudence did not say a word, but Josiah made his way to her with the doctor in a moment, where others were confused.

By the end of the day all Prudence and Faith could do was to hug each other by the morning room fire. The body had been tended and removed to the chapel of rest. Josiah had seen to that and sent word to the clerk of the mill that Prudence had declared there would be two days of mourning when the mill would be closed down, but the workers would still be paid, including the reinstated man, Bill.

She had asked Josiah to arrange for it to be cleaned before reopening and the books to be brought to her as soon as possible. In the rush of activity Josiah had forgotten to retrieve his cane which Prudence sat twirling in her fingers.

Benjamin joined them.

'It's finally over, Faith. We are free,' Prudence said quietly. 'You don't have to marry in haste if you do not wish to.'

'You do not have to marry at all . . . if you do not wish to, Faith.' Benjamin's words were said in a hushed voice.

Faith wrapped her arms around him. 'But I do, Benjamin, but not like this. After the funeral, we shall once we have sorted out that mill and cleaned up the workers' living quarters. Then everyone will have something to celebrate with us.'

Benjamin held her closely. 'You have some good ideas. Are you sure you need me?'

Faith kissed him, leaving him in no

doubt. 'We will put right years of wrong.'

'We could reduce the number of hours in a shift so that the people have time to rest, but increase the number of shifts by staggering the hours,' Benjamin said enthusiastically and Faith realised how much they thought alike.

Faith then turned to Prudence. 'But what of Letty?'

'She has a business and she is welcome to it.' Prudence saw Benjamin grin.

'I think you will find she has a partner as well now, the sign may read 'Rose & Bellowby, Milliners of distinction',' he answered.

'I hope so,' Faith said, as she took the cane out of her mother's hand.

'I must go and relay the news to them,' Benjamin said frankly and Prudence agreed. He left mother and daughter alone.

'So tell me, Mother,' she looked at the monogram engraved on the silver handle, 'What does the 'O' in Josiah O.

Baxter stand for?'

Prudence looked at Faith and then at the flickering flames of the fire and answered quietly, 'Oberon.'

'So I am 'Oberon's' child,' Faith said not knowing whether to feel shocked, ashamed or relieved that the man she loathed was not her true father.

'Yes, dear. I did not lie to you. But you see it was not I that could not conceive a son, it was he who could not have children. He would never have accepted that and, well, Josiah is such a lovely man. We . . . we . . . were in love.' Prudence flushed as she spoke.

'I believe you still are, Mother.' Faith held her mother's hand and the two sat quietly together by the fire's warmth contemplating the future they each now could have.

We do hope that you have enjoyed reading this large print book.

Did you know that all of our titles are available for purchase?

We publish a wide range of high quality large print books including:
**Romances, Mysteries, Classics
General Fiction
Non Fiction and Westerns**

Special interest titles available in large print are:
**The Little Oxford Dictionary
Music Book, Song Book
Hymn Book, Service Book**

Also available from us courtesy of Oxford University Press:
**Young Readers' Dictionary
(large print edition)
Young Readers' Thesaurus
(large print edition)**

For further information or a free brochure, please contact us at:
**Ulverscroft Large Print Books Ltd.,
The Green, Bradgate Road, Anstey,
Leicester, LE7 7FU, England.
Tel:** (00 44) **0116 236 4325**
Fax: (00 44) **0116 234 0205**

Other titles in the
Linford Romance Library:

THE SLOPES OF LOVE

Diney Delancey

Recovering from a broken engagement, Karen Miller takes a job as resort representative at St. Wilhelm in Austria. Working at the Hotel Adler, she finds herself constantly at odds with the owner, the cold and distant Karl Braun. The guests arrive for the Christmas and New Year holidays, but behind the jollity of the festivities lurks danger — a sinister threat reaching out from England — which Karen must face alone in the cold darkness of the mountain.